A bunch of zombie lunch ladies appeared at the shadowy end of the dining hall.

"I know them!" Zoe squealed. "That's Carol and Doris . . . and Darla . . . and Bertha."

Their faces drooped in pouches of wilted flesh like the back of an old person's elbow. Their frizzy perms fell in clumps from their hairnets. Bertha's eyes hung from their sockets by two twisty, blood-slathered tendons. The zombie lunch lady snagged an eyeball in each hand and stuffed them crisscrossed back into her face. *"Blaahrrgh!"* Big Bertha bellowed. The other lunch ladies hissed in response.

"What are we waiting for?" Ozzie raised his field hockey stick. "Get 'em!"

"Dude," Rice grabbed Ozzie's shoulder. "Never bite the hand that feeds you."

THE ZOMBIE CHASERS

UNDEAD AHEAD

BY JOHN KLOEPFER

ILLUSTRATED BY
STEVE WOLFHARD

HARPER

An Imprint of HarperCollinsPublishers

alloy**entertainment**

Produced by Alloy Entertainment
151 West 26th Street, New York, NY 10001

Library of Congress Cataloging-in-Publication Data
Kloepfer, John.
  Undead ahead / John Kloepfer ; [illustrations by Steve Wolfhard].
— 1st ed.
  p. cm. — (The zombie chasers ; #2)
  Summary: While trying to survive after zombies take over Phoenix,
Arizona, Zack, Rice, and Madison discover an antidote and embark on a
mission to save the nation from the zombie invasion.
  ISBN 978-0-06-185308-1
  [1. Zombies—Fiction. 2. Survival—Fiction. 3. Phoenix (Ariz.)—
Fiction. 4. Humorous stories.] I. Wolfhard, Steve, ill. II. Title.
PZ7.K8646Un 2011   2010033581
[Fic]—dc22   CIP
                                                              AC

                13 14 15   CG/BR   10 9 8 7 6
                              ❖
                  First paperback edition, 2011

For my mom and dad —J. K.

To Jake —S. W.

CHAPTER 1

Zack Clarke stood up in the back of the pickup truck, his pulse still beating fast from the getaway. The halogen lights buzzed overhead as the truck drove into the flickering blackness of the subterranean bunker.

The zombie outbreak had erupted yesterday around suppertime, sweeping across the country in a matter of hours.

Now, cruising beneath the Tucson Air Force Base, Zack's sister, Zoe, was still a zombie; his best friend, Rice, the self-proclaimed zombie expert, had figured out the zombie antidote; Greg Bansal-Jones, their school's most feared bully, had turned into a whiny sissy insisting that he was *not* Greg after his own brief zombification; and Madison Miller, the most popular girl at Romero Middle School, was their only hope for survival.

NotGreg squirmed away from zombie Zoe, who had been tranquilized by the dose of ginkgo biloba Rice had fed her a little less than an hour ago.

"Hey, man," NotGreg whimpered. "Will you untape me now?"

"Only if you keep quiet." Zack extracted the Swiss army knife from his back pocket and clipped the duct tape from NotGreg's wrists. The un-bully closed an imaginary zipper over his mouth, then threw away a make-believe key.

I can't believe I used to be scared of this dude, Zack thought, and peered inside the truck's cabin. Fresh blood soaked through the gauze stretched around the bite-wound on Madison's leg, a present from zombie Greg. Rice was riding shotgun with Madison's Boggle puppy, Twinkles, on his lap. Twinkles balanced his front paws on the dashboard, seeming happy to be alive again after a stint as a zombie mutt.

"How's the leg?" Zack asked Madison.

"Okay, I guess," she said. "I'm gonna kill Greg, though."

"You mean NotGreg."

"Whatever."

"Ah," said Rice. "To Greg or not to Greg? That is the question."

"Shut up, nerd burger," Madison said wearily. "Nobody's talking to you."

Just then, Twinkles nudged Rice's backpack with his snout, sniffing at the rank specimen within the bag.

Zack's stomach churned as he thought of the infected BurgerDog meat patty pulsating inside.

"Bow-wow-ow," the puppy howled hungrily.

"Hey, slow down, Madison," Zack said through the slider window, and the truck rolled to a stop.

On their right, the tunnel opened up into a large room, split into two levels by a loading dock. Yellow biohazard barrels lined the base of the high cement walls. A thick red splotch of zombie muck stained the square metal drain-grate in the center of the floor. The gory blotch extended into a curved smear that resembled a lowercase *j*. Uneven footprints were tracked around the ruddy trail of slime, as if the zombies had risen from a crawl.

The whole place reeked with the thick musk of disease, and Zack plugged his nose. Something was definitely rotten in Tucson.

"Eeeeee!" All of a sudden NotGreg let out a high-pitched squeal, grasping Zack's lower calf.

Zack whipped his head around.

A zombified soldier hung off the back of

the truck, climbing up the tailgate. The undead commando stretched its zombie yap, cobwebbed with spittle, wide open. It growled and gargled, wriggling its rabid tongue.

"Step on it, Madison!" Zack ordered.

Just then, two more zombie soldiers scaled the sides of the truck, tumbling into the cargo bed with Zack, NotGreg, and zombie Zoe. Their crooked limbs were set at impossible angles, like half-squashed daddy longlegs.

The pickup shot forward, full-throttle.

"Zack!" Rice called from inside the cab, and handed off a metal crowbar. "Use this!"

Zack flung the piece of iron at the zombie soldier, striking him between the empty sockets of his eyes. The tailgate fell open, and the eyeball-less madman dropped with a splat into the receding tunnel.

"*Blaahrrgh!*" the other two zombies bellowed.

Zack felt around frantically on the rumbling cargo bed for another weapon and found the wooden base of his Louisville Slugger.

Across the flatbed, one of the zombies crawled on dislocated kneecaps toward NotGreg. The terrified un-bully cowered in the corner by the open tailgate, his arms curled up like a Tyrannosaurus Rex's.

But Zack had his own problems.

The other zombie wheezed and tripped forward, fall-ing full-force on top of him. In a flash, Zack flipped the bat horizontal, his ears pulsing hotly, as he strained to bench-press the zombie upward. Bulbous viral clusters curdled and bulged off the chin of the diseased sicko, and tusks of yellow-green phlegm hung from the cor-ners of its raw swollen lips. The undead maniac grunted, and Zack felt his shoulder about to give. A ruptured infection dribbled off the zombie's cheek and onto the corner of Zack's mouth.

Puhtooey!

Zack heaved with every ounce of his strength, and the slobbering beast flung back, staggering to regain its balance. Zack stood up, holding the Slugger tight, ready to strike.

Suddenly, Madison shrieked at the top of her lungs, and the pickup lurched to a vicious halt.

Zack flew backward, bashing his head on the truck bed with a hard *thunk*.

"Dang, Madison!" Rice yelled inside the cab. "What'd you stop for?"

"Didn't you see?" she asked. "That person just jumped right out in front of us!"

"Zombies aren't people, Madison."

"It wasn't a zombie, dork brain . . . it was some little soldier-dude!"

Zack slumped down into a seated position, his ears ringing from the impact. His vision blurred and his head flopped sideways. Zack was looking directly at his zombified sister, Zoe. Her rolled-back, pupil-less eyes stared at him from behind the black metal cage of her facemask.

And as if fingers had snapped, Zack's mind went blank. Just like that.

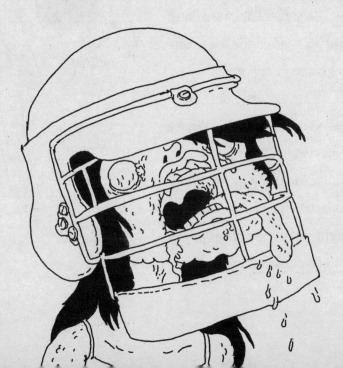

CHAPTER 2

ack awoke with a gasp. His nostrils burned
with the harsh tang of bleach. Someone was
standing over him, waving a bottle of stuff
under his nose.

"What is that?" Zack sat up, choking.

His eyes adjusted to the darkness, and a boy's wiry
figure gradually took shape. He wore a green long-
sleeved T-shirt, camouflage pants, and a heavy-looking
equipment pack strapped to his back.

"Smelling salts," the boy responded. "Carried by
doctors since the Middle Ages to revive flustered women
after they've fainted. Also known as ammonia chloride."

"I'm ammonia," Madison stated matter-of-factly.

"Oh, hello, Ammonia," NotGreg greeted her.

"No, Madison," Rice corrected. "You're immune."

"That's what I meant," she said.

Zack glanced past the new kid to where the two zombie soldiers were sitting back-to-back, knocked unconscious and expertly hog-tied with twine. "You did that?" he asked.

"Affirmative." The boy nodded. He had some kind of binoculars strapped to his head.

"Name's Ozzie Briggs."

"Zack, this dude's got night vision. Check it out." Rice pointed to the headpiece.

"Cool," Zack mumbled, rubbing the bump on his head.

"And nunchucks!" Rice reached for the martial arts weapon attached to Ozzie's pack.

"Hands off," Ozzie said. "The correct name for them is

'nunchaku.' They were a going-away present from my sensei in Okinawa."

"You're, like, a ninja turtle . . . ," Rice said, in awe of their new friend. He turned to Zack. "You should have seen it, man. This dude totally manhandled them! He came out of nowhere and was, like, *BAP BAP BAP*. . . ." Rice kicked his short little legs and tomahawked the air, miming the kung-fu zombie takedown.

"Yeah, and he almost killed us in the process," Madison said. "Who jumps out in front of cars like that, anyway?"

"Sorry about that, babe. I just react sometimes. And you all looked like you needed help."

Did he just call Madison 'babe'? Zack furrowed his eyebrows together. "Well, thanks for the help. . . ." He raised his arm for a handshake.

Ozzie ignored Zack's outstretched palm.

I can't believe this kid's really gonna leave me hangin', Zack thought. He dropped his hand and looked at his best friend quizzically, but Rice was still ninja-chopping away in the semidarkness of the tunnel.

"Can we go, you guys?" Madison asked. "My leg's starting to really hurt."

"She's right. We gotta get moving," Ozzie told them. "We're not really supposed to be down here."

"Wait, what about Zoe?" Madison asked.

"No way! My dad's got orders to exterminate these things!" Ozzie shouted.

"But we brought her all the way from Phoenix," said Rice.

"She's my sister, dude," Zack insisted. "We're not just going to leave her here."

"Yeah, *babe,*" Madison added. "Nobody messes with my BFF." She pronounced the word "biff."

"Fine . . ." Ozzie detached a neatly rolled blanket from his pack. "Bring her if you want, but if they see her, she's gonna be one dead zombie." Ozzie snapped the blanket open with a whip-crack, revealing a stretcher with two wooden handlebars at each end. Zack flinched. Rice punched his buddy's shoulder twice.

"What was that for?"

"Two for flinching." Rice smiled and skipped off next to Ozzie. He reached again for the nunchaku, but

Ozzie batted his arm away.

Rice pulled out a flashlight from his backpack and lit the way as they shuffled down the dark concrete passage. Zack and NotGreg carried Zoe on the stretcher. Madison limped along with Twinkles tucked snugly in the crook of her arm.

"So how'd you guys end up down here?" Ozzie asked, marching along easily with his night-vision goggles.

Rice began from the very beginning. "It all started after Zack hung up on me. I was sitting on my couch eating pizza skins when the news came on. Then— *BAM*—zombies were like everywhere!"

Ozzie led them up some steps and through a door that opened to a dark tunnel.

Rice went on. " . . . then after I saved these guys, they picked me up and we went to the supermarket to

get the ginkgo biloba, which I figured out can, like, slow down the zombification process or something."

"It also zonks them out, which is why Zoe's not moving and looks like a total creepo." Madison pointed at Zoe. "Poor BFF."

"Ahem." Rice nudged Ozzie. "So then at the graveyard, after the Gregster bit Madison, it was completely obvious that she was immune, and like—"

"Wait, Rice. Shhhh." Ozzie pressed his finger to his lips, and everyone paused. Up ahead, the sound of footsteps echoed through the tunnel. "Kill the flashlight," he whispered.

Rice flicked it off, encasing them in total blackness.

"I can't see anything," Madison whined.

"Rice, stop touching me!" said Zack.

"Wasn't me, dude," Rice said.

"Shhhh!" Ozzie shushed.

"Freeze!" A deep voice boomed in the dark.

Zack heard his sister's helmet clunk on the floor.

Just then, the ceiling lights buzzed and flickered, and the tunnel lit up. NotGreg was holding his hands in the air like a guilty felon.

A few yards in front of them, two soldiers stood in full camouflage. They wore big boots with shiny toes and carried automatic rifles slung over their shoulders. Their names were pinned on the breast pockets of their uniforms: MS PATRICK and PFC MICHAELS. Private Michaels had a crew cut and broad shoulders, and they both had very little in the way of a neck. Zack scooted himself in front of the stretcher to block Zoe from their line of sight.

"Ozzie?" Sergeant Patrick squinted. "What the heck are you doing inside my perimeter? Yer daddy's been lookin' all over for ya! Got 'im worried sick. . . ."

Private Michaels clicked his walkie-talkie and spoke into the receiver. "Strategic Command, this is Sub-Level A requesting the colonel."

A few seconds passed before a gruff, staticky voice crackled from the earpiece. "Briggs here."

"Colonel, this is Private Michaels down here in Sub-Level A with Sergeant Patrick. . . . We found your kid, sir. He's with some other kids, too, sir. . . . Don't know, sir. . . . You want to speak with him? . . . Copy that, sir."

Ozzie lifted his hand to take the walkie-talkie. Private Michaels clicked the button. "He'll speak to you later."

Just then, the stretcher started to twitch and snarl behind Zack's feet, and the soldiers switched their attention to what lay beneath the wriggling blanket. The sergeant brushed Zack out of the way with a rock-solid forearm, while the private squatted down next to the stretcher and unveiled the hideous beast.

"Oh, sweet Murphy!" Private Michaels cursed.

Zombie Zoe growled in a wild rage behind her lacrosse mask. Her face was cheese white with patches of skin that looked like tortilla chips. A creamy beige blob dripped from one corner of her mouth, looking like butterscotch fudge. Zack's stomach grumbled. He was hungrier than he thought.

"Put it out of its misery, Private," Sergeant Patrick ordered.

Private Michaels reached for his holster.

"Stop!" Zack yelled, jumping between zombie Zoe and Private Michaels. "You can't just kill her! That's my sister. . . ."

Zombie Zoe snorted and bucked, drooling as she snarled.

"Kid, that ain't nobody's sister—" Patrick gave her a sorry look.

"Boy, get out of the way!" yelled Michaels.

WHOOSH! At the end of the tunnel, a set of high-tech double doors shot open, and everyone froze.

CHAPTER 3

A hulking military officer sauntered toward them, backlit by the florescent glare of the hallway.

The sergeant, the private, and Ozzie all puffed out their chests and struck a stiff posture. Rice mimicked the soldiers, while Zack slouched wearily with his hands in his pockets. NotGreg sat cross-legged on the ground behind them and sighed. Madison shot the officer a tired peace sign and said, "Hey." Twinkles woofed.

"At ease," Colonel Briggs bellowed. "Now, what's going on?"

"Zombie smuggling, sir!" Sergeant Patrick announced, pointing at Zoe.

"Harboring zombies is a serious offense." The colonel's jaw flexed as he watched the zombified girl grunt and twitch.

"Son, we're in the middle of a zombie apocalypse, and you decide to break a direct order to screw around with these delinquent hooligans? I'm very disappointed in you, Oswald."

Ozzie kicked the dirt, mumbling curses.

"With all due respect, Mr. Colonel, sir," Rice interrupted, "your son saved our butts back there. And if it wasn't for him, we all might have been killed, and then there wouldn't be any more cure."

"Cure?" Colonel Briggs looked puzzled.

"That's right, Colonel," Rice continued. "Madison's a ginkgo biloba–infused super-vegan with serious antidote potential."

"Somebody better start makin' some sense," Briggs said. Rice opened his mouth to continue. "Anyone but you," said the colonel. He looked at Zack. "What about you, kid? Do you talk or what?"

Zack gulped. "Well, sir . . . Madison here was

bitten by zombie Greg, who was zombified by zombie Twinkles, who got zombified by a zombie burger—only Madison didn't zombify, because of the ginkgo. But then zombie Greg unzombified after biting her, and so did zombie Twinkles, which means that she's the zombie antidote. . . according to Rice."

The colonel stared blankly, then blinked. "Kid, I don't know what the zombie you're talking about, but that's just about the biggest whopper I've ever heard."

"Not Whoppers," Rice corrected. "BurgerDogs."

"BurgerDog?"

"It's that new fast-food joint, sir," said the Sergeant.

"You know: 'The burger that tastes like a dog,'" Private Michaels sang the advertising jingle.

"Yeah, exactly." Zack nodded quickly. "The burgers are carrying the zombie virus, but Madison's immune to zombification because she's a vegan and she drinks, like, tons of this ginkgo biloba water."

"Ginkgo baloney! It sounds to me like y'all evaded

mandatory inspection and trespassed on restricted government property."

Zoe let out a snot-strangled grunt.

"Why is that thing still sucking air, Sergeant?" Colonel Briggs asked.

Zack ran up to the colonel. "Sir, please, wait!"

"Young man, right now our top priority is eradicating every one of these brain-munchin' hell-demons

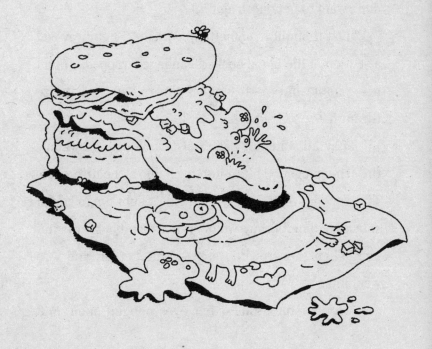

so the rest of us can survive."

Zombie Zoe snapped and gargled inside her protective headgear. "I mean, look at her." Briggs sighed. "It's a no-brainer."

"Permission to terminate, Colonel." Private Michaels reached for his weapon.

"Wait!" Madison shouted. "I'll prove it." She hobbled past the two soldiers. Briggs raised his eyebrows.

"Madison, what are you doing?" Zack asked. "You don't want to get bitten again."

"Just thought of something. Watch." She unraveled a section of the blood-soaked bandage wrapped around her zombie bite and dangled the red-stained gauze through Zoe's facemask.

They all watched Zack's sister chew and swallow the crimson gauze like a hungry llama at a petting zoo. The seconds plodded by, and Zoe's subhuman moan subsided. The bumpy welts on her face began to simmer. Then the growling stopped altogether, and Zoe went limp.

A few moments later her eyes popped open, and

her angry gaze settled on Zack. "You are dead meat, little bro!"

"Nuh-uh," NotGreg said. "You were the dead one. . . ."

"Shut up, Greg!" Zoe made an unpleasant face.

"That's NotGreg," Rice informed her.

"Yes, it is," she said sternly.

"No," Rice retorted. "It's Not."

"Just untie me," Zoe demanded, squirming furiously. Nobody moved. "Now!"

NotGreg scrambled to his feet, yanked off Zoe's chinstrap, and removed the helmet. He uncoiled the length of Mr. BowWow's leash that was wrapped around her body, and Zoe sat up.

"Sweet Moses!" the sergeant exclaimed. Colonel Briggs's mouth hung open as they both stared at the girl in disbelief.

"Why don't you guys take a picture?" Zoe snapped. "It'll last longer."

Colonel Briggs and Sergeant Patrick huddled up, muttering in the hushed tones of adults devising secret plans.

"OMG, Mad, what happened?" Zoe gasped at her BFF. "I mean, you look really bad."

Not as bad as you, Zack thought.

His sister's face was still covered with snarled patches of fungal rot, and her black bangs were matted to her forehead like the shiny jaws of some black desert beetle. But despite her bedraggled appearance and a few open sores, Zoe was completely human once again.

"I remember you being way prettier, Mad," Zoe went on rudely.

"You remember?" Rice asked.

"Of course I do, my little Johnston. . . ." Zoe was practically the only person who didn't call Rice by his last name. "I remember you being the nerdiest little nerd that ever nerded."

"She seems totally normal," Madison whispered to Zack.

"Oh yeah?" Rice shot back. "Well, you probably don't have any brain damage, because you'd have to have a brain for that."

Zoe raised her fist as if she was going to punch him. Rice recoiled and received two jabs in his upper arm.

"Listen, guys," Ozzie interrupted. "I don't mean to break up the reunion here, but my dad says we gotta get goin'. . . ."

A few floors and a couple of elevators later, they reached a small, locked room off a narrow hallway.

"Ten-hut!" Colonel Briggs stopped and pressed his right palm on a black touch screen that scanned his handprint. He then pressed his eyeball up to a retinal recognition scanner, and the door handle blipped green.

"Welcome, Colonel," a woman's futuristic voice greeted him.

Zack peeked inside, expecting something straight out of a sci-fi movie, but the room was no bigger than a utility closet and contained just a red rotary phone mounted on the wall. Colonel Briggs entered the room and extracted a silver chain with a single silver key from the front of his shirt. He flipped a few knobs on the switchboard and inserted the key into the old-school phone. Then he picked up the receiver and dialed three times: seven-seven-seven.

Clickclick-clickclick-clickclick-ding!

"This is Colonel Briggs requesting immediate Psy Ops rendezvous with Tucson AFB. . . . Uh-huh . . . We've got a little girl here who may be the key to this whole zombie fiasco. . . ." Colonel Briggs pinched his forehead and appeared to be deep in thought before launching into a complex series of code words: *Eagle. Phoenix. Panda. Godfather. Running Dog. Niner. Pancake.*

"What's going on?" Rice asked.

"Looks like he's callin' in the big boys," Private Michaels responded. "Your friend's going to Washington. Probably get to see the White House. . . maybe even meet the prez."

"Zack, I'm scared," Madison said meekly. The sergeant and the private were now carrying her on Ozzie's stretcher. "What are they gonna do with me?"

"Just wait and see what happens, okay? Everything's gonna be fine."

"Are you sure?"

No, Zack thought.

"Of course," he assured her.

"Roger that." The colonel hung up and turned to his men. "Take her down to medical and get her patched up before liftoff. I'll meet you on the helipad."

"Yes, sir!" They saluted in unison and started off down the hall with Madison.

"Wait!" Madison yelled, clutching Twinkles to her

chest. "Don't I even get to say good-bye?"

Colonel Briggs grunted, checking his watch. "Make it quick."

The whole gang crowded around Sergeant Patrick and Private Michaels.

"Thanks for saving me at Albertsons, Madison," Rice spoke first. "You were pretty cool tonight."

"Thanks, nerd." She held out her hand, balled into a fist. Rice gave her a pound and stepped away.

Now Zack stood in front of Madison.

"Zack, I don't know what to say." Madison looked at him, teary-eyed. "If it wasn't for you, we'd all be zombies right now. Well, maybe not me, but you know . . ." She put her arms out for a friendly hug, and Twinkles licked Zack's nose as he awkwardly embraced her.

NotGreg smiled and clasped his hands with approval, on the verge of happy tears. Zoe made a loud gagging sound.

"And Zoe," Madison addressed her BFF. "I know you think your brother's pretty lame . . . but he's not *that* bad."

Zoe nodded her head as if she finally understood. "You've lost a lot of blood, sweetie. And you're delusional, so I'll forgive you. Now I think you should let these nice hunky army guys take you to a doctor and make sure it's nothing permanent."

"All right, now," Colonel Briggs exhaled. "Does everyone feel all warm and fuzzy?" They all nodded. "Well, isn't that nice. Move out!"

"Good-bye, Ammonia." NotGreg frowned as the soldiers carted Madison and Twinkles away. "It was nice meeting you!"

CHAPTER

olonel Briggs led them quickly through the central corridor of the upper level. The hallway walls gleamed and sparkled, and Zack was glad to finally be someplace germless and sterilized.

The colonel stopped before another futuristic-looking entrance and inserted his key. The high-tech stainless-steel doors separated, and Colonel Briggs ushered them single file into the air traffic control room.

A large flat-screen was mounted above a giant control board. The monitor displayed six different squares, recording various angles from security cameras around the base.

Behind the digital console and video display, a curved prism of slanted glass overlooked the military complex. Outside, two enormous spotlights panned across the zombie-filled landscape. The undead hordes marched like drones across the desert flatlands, limping and staggering toward the security fences around the base. Zombies climbed over zombies, clawing at the crisscrossed metal barrier.

"All right, listen up!" Colonel Briggs bellowed from the doorway. His voice sent a shiver up Zack's spine. "This room is impenetrable. Do not even *think* about leaving without my say-so. Is that clear?"

"Yes, sir!" they replied.

"And don't touch *anything*," Colonel Briggs said brusquely. He turned and walked out of the room. The double doors slid automatically closed, and the kids were alone. The control room was quiet. NotGreg picked his nose.

"Your dad's mean," Zoe said, breaking the silence.

"He's just strict, that's all." Ozzie leaned over the console, peering at the security monitors.

Rice jumped into the seat behind the controls. "This place is sick! Just like in the movies." He twirled in the whirly-chair.

Just then, something buzzed, and Zoe jumped straight up. Her hip pocket was vibrating. "Ooh, goody! Texts!" She pulled out her cell phone. "I forgot all about you," she said, and gave it a kiss. "Excuse me, la-*hoo*-zers. I have to go be popular now."

Whoop-whoop-whoop!

All of a sudden the room lights dimmed. Red warning sirens blared and flashed in the top corners of the room.

"Uh-oh," Ozzie said. "That's not good."

"Wha-wha-what's not good?" NotGreg bit his fist.

"That!" Ozzie pointed at the security monitors.

Zack and Rice peered over Ozzie's shoulder, watching the display screens. A ferocious throng of zombified civilians piled up outside the barbed wire fences. Gray, flaking hands gripped the chain-link, shaking it violently. Eyeballs and fingertips littered the gravel.

"OMG, you guys!" Zoe called from the other side of the room. "Samantha Donovan ate Rachel Schwartz's face off!"

"Nobody cares!" Zack snapped at his sister.

Zack turned his attention back to the surveillance screen. Colonel Briggs and Sergeant Patrick were down on the runway with Madison, waiting for the chopper. Ozzie tapped a couple of buttons on the keyboard. The image zoomed and enhanced. The colonel screamed

orders into his walkie-talkie. Madison was wailing, trying to limp away. Sergeant Patrick snatched her with
one arm and tossed her over his shoulder. She kicked
the air and beat the sergeant's back with her fists, yell-
ing something at the top of her lungs.

Zack strained his eyes, trying to read her lips. It
looked like she was saying . . .

"Twinkles!" Rice shouted, pointing at the other split
screen. The security fence bent and toppled, and the tiny
pup darted heedlessly into the desert through a treacherous gauntlet of shuffling feet and bouncing eyeballs.

The warning siren continued to flash and blare
throughout the control room.

Zoe stepped behind the boys, scrolling through her in-box. "Jamie Dumpert has no eyeballs . . . Hah!" She let out a goofy guffaw, clicking through her zillionth text message. "O . . . M . . . G!"

"Zoe, I swear if you even say one more—"

"This one's from Mom and Dad, turd breath!" Zoe cut Zack off.

"What? What does it say?" Zack asked.

"Oh, I see." Zoe paused. "Now you're interested in my popularness."

"Zoe!"

His sister cleared her throat. "It says: 'Dearest daughter, we love you so. We always will. It's time for your brother to know the truth. Zack . . . is adopted.'"

"Shut up, Zoe," Zack grumbled.

She clicked another button. "It's a video text, dweeb-azoid. . . ."

"When did they send it?" he asked.

"Half hour ago," Zoe replied.

They're still alive . . . , he thought.

The video took a few seconds to load. Zack watched over his sister's shoulder as their parents' grainy faces appeared on the tiny digital screen. They were huddled under a desk, half in shadow. The video message settled on a shaky handheld close-up of Mrs. Clarke's face. Her voice was hushed and difficult to hear through the low-quality audio.

" . . . Is it going? . . . I don't know. . . . Kids? We're still at school. . . . We want you to know that we love you . . . and if we make it out of here, this will definitely be our last parent-teacher night." A loud crash

sounded in the background. "Did you hear that? . . . Shhhhh . . ."

The screen went black.

A feeling of dread expanded in the pit of Zack's stomach. *Were his mom and dad okay?* There was only one way to find out. . . .

But just then, a bright dazzle of light beamed down through the windows. "What is that?" Zoe asked as the spotlight passed overhead.

"It's here!" Ozzie shouted. "The chopper!" They leaned over the console, watching the monitors.

The jet-black helicopter hovered above the zombie-laden runway. A rope ladder

dropped into view, swaying a few feet over the center of the landing pad. Madison scanned the zombie-infested landscape for her lost puppy as she climbed shakily to the top rung, where two men in dark suits and sunglasses pulled her safely aboard. The chopper lifted into the black, star-spangled sky.

"Yay!" NotGreg shouted. He jumped onto one of the whirly-chairs, zooming around with his arms out, pretending to be an airplane. Zack watched as the rolling chair suddenly tipped backward, and NotGreg bashed his chin against the control board before landing on the floor with a thud.

Another loud buzzer sounded, and a woman's calm, digitized voice came over the air force base's alert system. "Three minutes until automatic lockdown. Repeat. Three minutes . . ."

"You moron!" Ozzie cussed, tapping frantically at the keyboard.

NotGreg's head tilted to the side. His eyes shut and he conked out on the floor. Zack knelt down, trying to shake him awake.

"Ozzie," Zack said. "Do that thing you did to me with the smelly salts."

"Those were all I had. . . ." He grimaced.

"Whoa!" Rice pointed at the security cams. On-screen, Sergeant Patrick and Colonel Briggs were still down on the airstrip. They were surrounded, trapped in a thick ring of converging zombies. The colonel and the sergeant fought bravely, throwing punches, side by side.

Ozzie gulped, his eyes widening.

Zack felt nauseous, thinking about his own mom and dad trapped in a school full of zombies.

Just then, the sputtering sound of gunfire muttered through the walls. "What was that?" Rice asked. They whipped their heads around and scanned the surveillance monitors.

A massive pack of zombie freaks stormed through the military complex, clogging up a four-way corridor. Private Michaels knelt in the intersection, scrambling to reload. He smacked in his last ammo cartridge, but the thick crowd of zombies mauled the private before he could get a shot off.

"Dang!" Ozzie swore. "They're on our floor."

"How'd they get up here so fast?" Zack asked, a slight panic in his voice.

"I don't know," Ozzie said. "But they're here."

Zack's eyes wandered back to the display screen that showed the helipad. A dense swarm of mutated lunatics filled the monitor. No sign of the colonel or the sergeant.

"Two minutes until automatic lockdown," the robot voice warned.

"You guys, we have to get out of here. . . ." Zack replayed the video over again in his mind. "We've got to get back to Phoenix and save our parents."

"What about NotGreg?" Zoe asked. "He's too cute to get eaten."

NotGreg sucked his thumb, knocked out on the cold, hard floor.

"He'll be safe here. You heard what my dad said," Ozzie told them.

"Then what are we waiting for?" Zack asked.

"But we do things my way. Got it?" shouted Ozzie.

"Got it!" Rice yelled.

"Got it," Zack mumbled.

"Whatever you say, hotness." Zoe smacked the automatic button on the wall, and the doors opened. "Let's go!"

CHAPTER 3

White emergency lights flashed like strobes overhead, as Zack, Rice, Ozzie, and Zoe raced into the corridor. A thick pack of mangled arms and legs surged around the corner, as a decaying heap of bowlegged zombies funneled into the linoleum hall.

"Other way!" Zack shouted.

They doubled back, skidding around the opposite corner. At the far end, a second ghastly gaggle of zombies jam-packed the hallway, heading straight for them. They were trapped, caught between two slow-motion droves closing in on both fronts.

"Shoot!" Zack shouted. "What do we do?"

"I'll handle this," Ozzie said, unhooking the nun-chaku from the metal clasp on his army pack.

"Dude, you better be Bruce Lee if you're planning to fight through all those things," Zack said. He stared past Ozzie at the gruesome horde tottering psychoti-cally down the corridor. The zombies groaned, retching up slime as they waddled forward. A haze of stench hov-ered around them, filling the hallway with the rotten stink of death.

Zoe dashed to the only door on the hallway and yanked it open. "Stupid closet!"

"What's in it?" Zack brushed his sister out of the way.

A yellow bucket filled with old filthy water and a mop stood next to two push brooms in the corner. Zack grabbed a detergent bottle off the shelf, squeezed some soap into the nasty bilge water, and swished the suds around with the mop. "Here." He handed the brooms to Zoe. "Give one to Rice."

Behind them, the first mob of zombies stumbled and crawled their way up the hall. In front of them, the second herd of toothless, drooling goons staggered down the corridor.

Zack lifted the dripping mop head out of the bucket and soaked the floor.

"What are you doing?" Zoe asked. "You're just making it slippery."

"That's the idea, genius," Zack said, mopping backward. "Nice and soapy."

"I get it . . . ," Ozzie said, running up to the yellow bucket. "But we need to speed things up. We've got under a minute to get out of here." He kicked it sideways.

"What the—?" Zack shouted.

The bucket tipped, and the soapy liquid spilled at the feet of the zombie stampede. The beastly brood stepped into the expanding puddle of mop water and slipped on the slick linoleum like first-time ice skaters. They pawed at the walls for balance, only to slide and crumple.

"Follow my lead." Ozzie gripped his nunchaku and took off, sliding through the tumbling

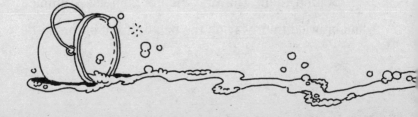

ghouls. With two quick whaps, Ozzie clobbered two of the zombies, then spun backward like a hockey defenseman, clocking two more. He finished with a well-timed reverse back flip over the last zombie and landed onto the dry floor.

Who is this kid? Zack thought.

"Ready . . . set . . ." Zack clutched the mop handle. The zombies were three feet behind them, making noises like cartoon people eating: *Nom nom nom.*

"Go!" Zoe lunged forward, head-hunting for fallen fiends with her push broom, while Rice raced through the zombies covering the floor. Zack used the mop to pole-vault over the reanimated slip-'n'-slimers. On the other side, Ozzie was in the clear, knocking zombies out one by one until there were none left.

"Thirty seconds until automatic lockdown . . . ," the voice warned them.

"Hurry," Ozzie called out over the blaring alarm. "We can still make it in time!" He led the way through the dim crimson pulse of the base, stutter-stepping down a cement stairwell with Zack, Zoe, and Rice close behind.

"Automatic lockdown will begin in ten, nine, eight . . ."

Ozzie slid down the handrail and crashed into the push-bar of the emergency exit door.

" . . . three . . . two . . one . . ."

Reaching the ground floor, they all hustled outside.

"Lockdown complete," the robot lady announced as the door bolted behind them. They stood on a small

cement staircase, staring out over a sea of motor vehicles.

"What are all these cars doing right here?" Zoe asked.

"Must be from the traffic jam," Zack said.

"I don't remember a traffic jam," Zoe said.

Rice reminded her. "When you were all . . ." He hunched his neck and clawed at the air, making a zombie face. "In the back of your mom's Volvo."

In the distance, hundreds of zombie savages limped across the tarmac, gurgling their own mucus.

"Get down!" Ozzie ordered as he hit the deck.

Crawling on all fours, Zack heard an ungodly groan and peeked under a Jeep Wrangler to his right. A zombie policewoman squirmed on its stomach, scraping itself along the gravel. It jerked its head to the side and glared at Zack. Its bloodshot eyes were solid pink. The zombified female cop smiled eerily, wheezing through its open mouth. It slithered after them, wedging its body

under the Jeep, growling and snorting.

"Move it, Rice!" Zack yelled as he scrambled into a run like a sprinter off a starting block.

They stopped at the last car, peering over the front of a purple Cadillac with long bull's horns mounted on the hood. A crisscrossing death trap of cantankerous fiends lumbered past the rows of cars. Hairy-chested zombie men with earrings sputtered mouthfuls of teeth. Willowy zombie women staggered along, their veiny skin dripping from their bent and broken forearms. Little old lady zombies in bathrobes and slippers tottered next to undead cowboys in ten-gallon hats, limping in their leather boots, spurs jangling with each off-kilter step. Brains leaked out of nostrils. Skin flaked in great, disintegrated hunks. Each zombie was more revolting than the one before.

Ozzie pointed past the undead bedlam. A large army tank sat by the security fences, where more zombies stumbled in from the scrubland. "I hope you guys are feeling limber," he said, stretching his quads and arching his back.

"You wanna go through that?" Zoe asked blankly.

"Yeah, what's the matter?" Ozzie looked Zoe over. "You look like you're in good shape." He cocked his head at the boys. "It's these two I'm nervous about."

"What's that supposed to mean?" Zack asked.

"The two of you don't exactly look like you play a lot of sports. . . ." Ozzie let the insult hang in the ripe-smelling air.

"Whatever, dude. We were doing just fine before you showed up," Zack scoffed.

"All right. All right. Everybody just be cool." Ozzie

grabbed his nunchaku off his pack. "And don't get in my way."

Ozzie approached the brain-dead frenzy, swinging the nunchaku slowly.

The zombies' bulging heads rotated toward them as they entered the shambling footslog of the living dead. Ozzie sprang into action and unleashed a furious attack, clearing a path for the rest of them. The only sound was the *whizz* of wood whipping through the air and the meaty *thwacks* of serious skull trauma courtesy of Ozzie's dazzling nunchaku freestyle.

The brainsick psychos dropped to the concrete in ones and twos. Zack, Rice, and Zoe bobbed and weaved across the runway, dodging flailing zombie limbs. As soon as they reached the clearing, Rice and Zoe raced for the great black tank. Zack was about to follow when he saw the last zombie shuffling toward Ozzie.

Colonel Briggs stood before his son, missing an arm. Blood spurted out from the bony nubbin of his shoulder as if it were a ketchup squeeze bottle.

"Dad?" said Ozzie, losing his grip on the nunchaku.

They sailed through the air, clattering on the cement. "Your arm!"

The zombie colonel waggled his dismembered limb by the wrist like a caveman waving a club. Ozzie froze as his father raised his good arm, preparing to clobber his son with the severed appendage.

Zack charged from a standstill and tackled Ozzie to the ground. The colonel lost his balance, falling to the pavement with a thud. As the zombie arm whiffed by their heads, the boys rolled out of danger and scrambled to their feet.

"What's the matter with you?" Ozzie gave Zack a shove like a chest-pass without the basketball. "I said don't get in my way!"

"Fine," Zack said angrily. "Next time your dad wants to play T-ball with your head, I'll let the two of you bond." He rubbed his collarbone, sore from Ozzie's shove. Ozzie stood still, looking back at Colonel Briggs, who was on the ground, slithering toward them. The colonel's zombutated arm crawled next to him like the Addams Family's pet, Thing.

Ozzie glared at his old man, his eyes welling with tears, as the massive herd of zombies started to shift in their direction, about to trample over his dad.

"Come on—let's go!" Ozzie's voice cracked a little.

And with that, they raced to the armored tank, friend and foe, as the zombies stumbled relentlessly toward them.

CHAPTER

Ozzie sat in the driver's seat, studying a row of primary-colored buttons. He twisted the throttles and hit the green one that read DRIVE ACTION. The tank rattled and rolled forward, plowing through the zombie-laden perimeter.

Zoe sat behind the periscope lens for the turret cannon. Zack sat next to Rice on the seat bench bolted to the wall. Black-and-white curlicue cables drooped down from the low ceiling of the cramped tank. The rear hutch was filled with hydraulic valves and nozzles, black handles with little red trigger buttons, and vents and compartments plastered with orange caution stickers and warning labels.

"Here, take these and go up top." Ozzie reached back into the crawl space compartment and pulled out two sets of night-vision goggles. "Try and spot the highway."

"Sweet!" Rice took the headgear and strapped it on. His ears sprouted oddly from the elastic headband. He grinned, looking a bit dweebish.

Zack put the headgear on and climbed up through the turret hatches, scanning the landscape. The tank was headed straight for a steep hillside, where a barrage of zombies stumbled down the craggy slope, wreathed in a lime-colored mist. They pulsed and throbbed in the night vision's green neon flare.

Zack ducked his head down through the hatch. "Hard left, Oz!" He popped back up as the tank swung left, nearly sideswiping the zombified foothill.

"That was close." Zack wiped his brow.

Just then a zombie, looking as ragged as a homeless person, bounded at the tank and rode up the giant rolling tread as if it were a conveyer belt. The rabid hobo raised its limp-wristed arms, Z-shaped, and let out a wretched snarl.

"Zack, watch out!" Rice yelled over the tank's loud rumble.

The undead vagabond pounced off the grooved tread, and Zack leaned away as the stringy-haired beast fell hard on the desert floor. *Phew!*

Zack panned across the horizon just over the moonlit gloom of the foothills. He spotted a cement overpass that looked as though it looped onto the freeway. The boys ducked back down into the tank.

"The highway's right up there, Ozzie," Zack told him. "Dead ahead."

Back inside, Rice looked around, sniffing the air, like a kitten watching a flying insect. "What's that smell?" he asked. "Do you smell that?"

"You mean Zoe?" Zack snickered.

Rice sucked in hard through his nostrils. "It's

BurgerDog," he declared finally.

Zack breathed in the rotten hot dog flavor, too. Rice was right. "Are you sure it's not the one in your bag?"

"The baggie is airtight," Rice confirmed.

"Wait a sec. . . ." Zack climbed back up through the turret hatch.

He gazed out into the predawn night. A dome of blue neon light bloomed off the side of the road up ahead.

Zack activated the zoom function on his night-vision goggles.

A gigantic revolving BurgerDog dachshund twirled slowly above a highway rest stop. A trickle of smoke rose from the kitchen in the rear. The parking lot was piled up with abandoned vehicles. Head-on collisions and fender benders were logjammed at odd angles throughout the lot. Smashed windshields were smeared with rancid sludge. The front of the fast-food place was trashed. A small fire blazed at the self-service pump, where a car had barreled into one of the gas tanks.

"Arf!" A tiny dog bark echoed through the eerie stillness. Zack listened again. *Was he hearing things?* "Arf! Arf!"

Twinkles?

"Ozzie, pull this thing over!" Zack yelled from above.

Ozzie veered the tank off the highway,

pulling into the post-apocalyptic junkyard. ZOMBEEZ! was scrawled in the grimy film on the side panel of a Ford pickup. The blacktop squirmed with squiggling clusters of desert rodents, all vying for strewn scraps of burger meat.

Rice and Zoe climbed out the hatch after Zack, while Ozzie hopped out of the driver's hole. They jumped down and ran through the floor of squealing vermin toward the BurgerDog entrance, where Twinkles was barking up a storm.

"Ugh!" Zoe exclaimed as a rat ran over her foot. "I wish I wore my Uggs!"

"Twinkles!" Zack yelled, and ran toward the pup.

Ozzie stopped dead in his tracks and pointed at the ground. "Snake . . ."

A BurgerDog-stuffed zombie rattlesnake snapped

its gangrenous fangs at the stubborn mutt.

Twinkles growled, defending his half-nibbled BurgerDog patty from the zombified serpent. The puppy put his head down near its front paws, raised his hindquarters, and wagged his tail. "Arf!" He thought they were playing.

Hissss . . . kchaaa. Tsssss! Apparently, the zombie snake did not.

Suddenly, the bulge in the middle of the snake sprouted little scraggly feet and claws, ripping out through the innards of the reptile. It was a hideous reversal of consumption and digestion, rebirth and undeath—the food chain gone kooky.

"Sick," Rice said, entranced by the unnatural disorder of things.

The zombie snake thrust its wide, jawless mouth over the rat hatching from its belly, busy eating the same meal for a second time.

Twinkles gagged, yacking up zombie hot-dog burger meat. Zack swooped in and snatched up the pooch. He scratched Twinkles behind the ears. "You shouldn't have eaten that. . . ."

The puppy swiveled his head around, squeaking out sad little whimpers.

"What's the matter? You miss Madison?" And it was then that Zack looked up and saw what was making Twinkles squeal.

A zombie truck driver lumbered out from behind his tipped eighteen-wheeler. Then a BurgerDog drive-through worker rose up behind a smashed red convertible, his potbelly drooping ogrelike over his shredded trousers. More and more zombies appeared out of the wreckage. Half-dead road-trippers and junk-food eaters, slime-slathered soccer moms and grease-soaked gas station attendants, all moaning for brains. The rest-stop zombies stumbled through the rat-infested parking lot, casting their demented gaze upon the little dog's rescuers.

"Dude," said Rice. "I think we just got put on the dollar menu."

"Retreat!" Ozzie shouted.

They took off in a mad dash for the tank.

Zoe screamed as a massive swarm of undead rats gathered up fast around their feet. Her cell phone clattered on the blacktop. "My baby!" She stopped, looking back, as the hissing, squealing rodents engulfed the wireless device.

"Forget about your stupid phone, Zo!" Zack grabbed his sister by the arm, pulling her away from the carpet of squirming fur.

They quickly climbed up the hull of the tank and hopped inside. The tank rattled and started to roll, and as Ozzie pulled the vehicle back onto the highway, Zack listened to the bony squish and squeal of zombie rats caught in the gears.

"Got everyone?" Ozzie called back.

Rice did a quick headcount. "Aye, aye, cap'n!"

"Arf! Arf!" Twinkles barked, trying to lick Zack's face.

"You're welcome," Zack told the black-and-white pup. And the tank merged onto the four-lane freeway filled with the living dead limping on bent and twisted limbs, shuffling across the blacktop.

CHAPTER

inally, they were back on Zack's, Rice's, and
Zoe's home turf.

For more than two hours, Ozzie had steered
the tank through the desert night, waxing autobio-
graphical. Zack had met Ozzie only a few hours ago, and
he already knew the kid's entire life story.

Martial arts training. Jungle safaris. Scuba diving.
He could drive a tank. He knew kung fu. What else was
there? Could he fly a plane? Zack wondered if he could
fly *without* a plane. It seemed possible if he had a little
superhero cape.

The tank rumbled to a stop next to a yellow sign that

warned: SLOW! CHILDREN AT PLAY.

They climbed out of the tank and hopped down in the crosswalk. At the end of the street, a curtain of shadow dropped down the front of Romero Middle School as the sun rose over the horizon.

Everything seemed fine. The parking lot was full of minivans, as neat and pretty as a car dealership. The flower beds and bushes lay untrampled in the bird-chirping quiet. The exterior of the school was intact except for a single broken window and the burnt-rubber tread marks of a getaway van. The tire tracks swerved across the lawn. *Maybe Rice's parents actually got away,* Zack thought. Or were the Rices devouring Zack's mom and dad this very instant?

"Mom!" Zack shouted as they approached the school building.

"Dad!" Zoe called.

"Arf!" Twinkles barked.

Ozzie breathed deeply through his nose. "I love the smell of zombies in the morning."

The five of them cast long shadows on the stone steps as they reached the main entrance. They cupped their hands against the window glass, staring inside the lobby of the school.

WHAM!

A putrid zombie arm shot straight through the windowpane, grabbing Rice by his pock-speckled face. It was Senora Gonzalez, their Spanish teacher. The senora reached through the armhole of jagged shards.

"*AHHHHHHH!*" Rice jumped back, and his glasses fell on the cement step. "I can't see!" He squinted, grabbing at the air in front of him like a zombie.

Senora Zomzalez glared at Rice with a wild-eyed scowl. "*Adios, Arroz!*" the zombie gurgled moistly. Its grunts steamed up the window as it tried to gnaw through the pane of glass.

Zack picked up his buddy's glasses, and Rice put them back on. "Aw, man, they got a crack." Rice shook his finger at his former teacher. "No es bueno, Senora G. Es muy mal."

"If we go in there, we're gonna need to find some weapons first," Ozzie told them.

"What about the equipment room off the soccer field?" Zack suggested.

"It's probably locked." Rice pouted.

"Locks are not a problem," Ozzie said casually, and so they hustled around to the back of the school.

Across the football field, two zombie lacrosse players were hobbling around, cradling eyeballs in the pockets of their sticks and whipping them at each other four at a time.

"Ewww!" Zoe shrieked.

"Shhhh!" Rice shushed her to a whisper. "Zack, will you please tell your sister the first rule of zombies?"

"Don't let the zombies bite you, Zo," Zack said. "Oh, wait, you already did!"

"No, the other rule . . ." Rice waited, but Zack stared at him blankly.

"Zombies are attracted to sound, bro."

"That's not a rule, that's a fact," Zoe said. "You don't know anything about zombies. I, on the other hand, have first-hand experience."

"Be quiet!" Ozzie said as they reached the red double doors of the equipment room. He pulled out a thin metal tool from his pack. "This'll just take a minute."

Zack sighed and glanced out across the other sports fields in back of the school. A headless soccer player juggled its missing noggin like a ball. The zombie planted its weak foot and blasted a shot on goal. The decapitated head rocketed off the cleat and *doinked* the crossbar. It wobbled to a stop on the goal line, and the body crumpled on the damp morning grass. No goal.

"Uhh, Rice? I thought you said they die if you cut their heads off," Zack said.

"Errr, I—I can't explain that one." Rice stuttered a little. "That's just weird."

A few minutes later, Zoe tapped her foot and

checked an invisible watch on her
wrist. Rice yawned. It was way past
his sleepytime.

Just then, a low guttural growl
gurgled behind them. They turned
to see the headless sportsman drib-
bling its decapitated noggin between its cleats. All of a
sudden, the beheaded ghoul chipped its noggin up
off the grass. *"Blurgle-dahrgh!"* The decapitated zombie head lobbed high in the air, heading right toward
them, biting its own tongue over and over as it soared
overhead.

"Ewww, hurry!" screeched Zoe.

"Got it!" Ozzie cracked the lock.

The door popped open, and Ozzie scurried into
the equipment room.

"Get in!" Zack shooed Rice, Zoe, and Twinkles inside,
then dove in after them and slammed the door shut.

Zack heard a juicy thud as the flying noggin
smacked outside the equipment room and dropped
to the ground with a snarl.

Zack flipped the light switch on. The room was zombie free.

"Listen," said Zoe, gazing at the ceiling.

Tortured moans and zombie howls echoed through the air vents.

"Mom and Dad are up there," Zoe said solemnly.

"Come on, guys," Zack said. "We need to get moving,"

They gathered supplies and geared up for the coming battle.

Rice and Zack fitted each other with football shoulder pads and baseball catcher's vests. Zack uncapped a little tin of baseball grease and wiped a black smudge under each eye. Next, he went over to a wooden barrel filled with assorted baseball bats and picked out a gleaming aluminum Slugger. It was officially his weapon of choice.

Rice put on a lacrosse helmet. "Who am I?" he asked. "'Zack, blaah, I hate you, blaah, I'm gonna eat you, blaahhhhhh.'" He pointed at Zoe and laughed. "I'm you!"

Zoe unsheathed a hockey stick from another barrel and whapped Rice hard on his helmeted head.

"Guys, get serious," Ozzie said. He was wearing elbow pads and strapping multiple shin-guards around each calf.

Zack held up two football helmets. He put one on and tossed the other to Ozzie.

"No need," he said. "But thanks."

"Suit yourself." Zack prac-ticed his batter's stance.

Twinkles sniffed a crusty pair of forgotten socks in a dusty corner.

Ozzie pulled a batter's glove onto each hand and grabbed a field hockey stick. Zoe put on a fresh pair of soccer goalie gloves, clapping her new mitts together. She hopped back in a funny stance like a fighting Irishman and socked Zack in the helmet as hard as she could.

"Oww!" he yelped.

"Put up your dukes, dork!"

"Zoe, knock it off!"

"Wrong choice of words, Broseph." She punched him again, and his head snapped back. "Hah! Fun-ness."

On the other side of the room, Rice picked up a red-and-white plastic bullhorn from a box and attached it to his pack. Zack shot his friend a wary glance. "What?" Rice asked. "It might come in handy."

"You know you have a history with those things. . . ."

"They're fun," Rice said innocently. "I mean, useful."

"You guys ready to roll?" Ozzie asked.

"One second." Rice finished putting on some knee-pads and grabbed a field hockey stick for himself.

All of a sudden, Zoe shrieked.

She was standing in front of a mirror for the first time since her unzombification. "Eeee-you," she said quietly, inspecting her reflection. "How can you even look at me? I'm hideous!" Tears streamed down her horrified face.

Zack, Rice, and Ozzie looked at one another and shrugged.

Zoe sniffled and stared off into space. "Someone

better tell me I'm beautiful before I pass out," she said.

Nobody peeped.

"Quick, I'm feeling faint."

"Uh," Zack said, "you're . . . beautiful?"

"Yeah, Zoe," Rice said. "You, you're the prettiest."

"*LIARS!*" Zoe screeched. "You liars make me sick." She pinched and prodded her crusty, curdled face and then took a deep breath. "As long as Ozzie knows that I'm usually way cuter than this . . ." Then she found a hockey helmet with a tinted visor and put it on to hide her hideousness from the world.

And just like that, they rolled out of the equipment room to rescue Mr. and Mrs. Clarke.

Either that or go clock them in the head.

CHAPTER 8

They navigated cautiously through the dark first floor of the middle school. A soda machine cast a faint red glow at the end of the corridor.

Zack, Zoe, Rice, and Ozzie walked on soft, cat feet across the black-and-white checkered linoleum. Twinkles scampered along, too, but on puppy feet.

All of a sudden the dog froze, sniffed the air, and then took off running.

"Twinkles!" Zack called, chasing after the pup. They caught up with him next to the vending machine, where the janitor's office door hung slightly ajar. Ozzie kicked it open with his foot. The rusty hinges creaked loudly.

"Dude . . . ," Zack whispered.

"My bad," Ozzie said.

"Look, you guys." Rice pointed from the doorway.

Inside the office, two half-eaten BurgerDog value meals lay open on the desktop. Twinkles pranced happily around the fast food. "The outbreak must have happened inside," Rice realized.

"Poor parents," Zoe sympathized. "Where do you think they are?"

"*If* they are . . . ," Ozzie added cynically.

"Zack, if you were your parents, where would you be?" Rice asked.

"In the principal's office," Zack said with certainty.

"How do you know?"

"It's the place they visit most often," Zack explained, recalling all the times his parents had been called there to discuss his extracurricular activities. Like selling horror comics to fifth-graders. Or getting caught with Rice after tipping the Coke machine for free sodas. Or talking too much in Senora G.'s Spanish section. "Maybe your parents are there, too."

"Makes sense." Rice nodded, a serious look on his face.

They approached another hallway and turned the corner slowly, tiptoeing toward the cafeteria. Meaty globs of freak tissue were smeared all over the puke-green lockers. The walls were tacked with class projects and school banners, all slathered in some kind of egg-whitey pus.

A student council campaign poster with big bubble letters and money symbols read: VOTE 4 GREG—OR HE'LL BREAK YOUR LEG! It, too, was dripping in slime. In the picture, Greg Bansal-Jones smiled, giving himself two thumbs way up.

Just then, a faint zombie howl reverberated through the shadowy beige hallway. "Did you hear that?" Zoe asked.

The doors to the cafeteria swung back and forth, creaking on their hinges.

Zack smelled the permanent stink of stale milk and old mac-and-cheese wafting into the hall.

"Hello?" Rice whispered as they pushed through

the swinging doors. "Zombies?"

The mess hall was a serious mess. Long lunch tables were tipped or pushed at awkward angles, and stacks of plastic chairs were toppled, sculpture-like, around the cafeteria. Racks of unrefrigerated leftovers were knocked over, spilling into spoiled puddles of yesterday's goulash and bread pudding.

Zack couldn't believe it. This room had been spotless when he left it after yesterday's detention. All that hard work for nothing!

Suddenly, Twinkles growled his little growl, and they all looked up. A bunch of zombie lunch ladies appeared at the shadowy end of the dining hall.

"I know them!" Zoe squealed. "That's Carol and Doris . . . and Darla . . . and Bertha."

VOTE 4 GREG
$ $ $
$
OR HE'LL BREAK YOUR LEG!

Their faces drooped in pouches of wilted flesh like the back of an old person's elbow. Their frizzy perms fell in clumps from their hairnets. Bertha's eyes hung from their sockets by two twisty, blood-slathered tendons. The zombie lunch lady snagged an eyeball in each hand and stuffed them crisscrossed back into her face. *"Blaahrrgh!"* Big Bertha bellowed. The other lunch ladies hissed in response.

"What are we waiting for?" Ozzie raised his field hockey stick. "Get 'em!"

"Dude," Rice grabbed Ozzie's shoulder. "Never bite the hand that feeds you."

Big Bertha and the other lunch ladies lumbered slowly toward them through the sloppy mess hall.

Suddenly Mr. Fred, the assistant custodian, staggered out of the girls' bathroom. He lurched shoulder-first into Zack, who dropped his bat. The aluminum clank resounded off the walls.

The reanimated janitor leered into Zack's football helmet, ogling him with the strange, fixed grin of a psycho killer. Crazy Fred thrust his head down, mouth agape, baring brown, blood-slickered teeth. It looked as though he'd just been chewing gobs of chocolate.

"Help!" Zack screamed.

The zombie janitor's tongue was canker-blistered and freckled with black bacteria. Zack pushed the ghoul's drooling face away with his bare hand. His index finger slipped into the zombie's wet, slime-encrusted nostril.

"Help!" Zack cried once more, ready to puke. A mucusy driblet hung off the face mask, almost touching the tip of Zack's nose.

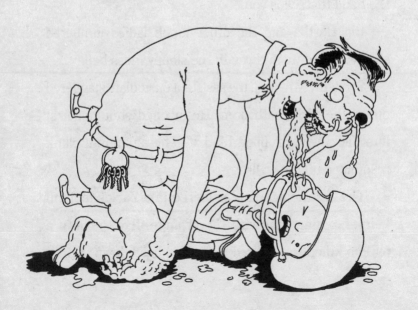

Finally, a hand swooped down and grabbed the slobbering beast by the hair. The zombie janitor reeled back, pawing at the air. Ozzie's arm flew back with a handful of slimy hair attached to a jagged piece of scalp. Rice took a hard cut at the maintenance man with his field hockey stick. The blow connected with a *splat*, and the big, mannish beast slunk down, limp and still.

Ozzie and Rice bumped chests and growled like lions.

Zack jumped to his feet and brushed himself off quickly. "Thanks, guys." He wiped the nostril goop onto his pants.

"No sweat," Ozzie replied. "I owed you one."

Zoe dragged a long table between them and the lunch ladies, who were still shuffling their way. She grabbed the edge and flipped up one side of the table, tipping it over like a barricade.

"Good idea, Zoe!" Ozzie threw the clump of zombie hair on the floor and ran over to help.

The zombie lunch ladies were getting closer. Ozzie pulled over another table, creating a wide blockade.

Zack and Rice dragged a mess of chairs behind the tables to reinforce the barrier.

Zombie Darla was holding a whisk dripping with what looked like cake batter. She flailed her arm and spattered Zoe's face with clumps of yellow mix.

"Yuck!" screeched Zoe, who picked up a pink cupcake and launched it across the room, where it exploded with a *splat* on zombie Carol's apron.

"Food fight!" Rice shouted, scooping a handful of bread pudding off the floor and flinging it at Zoe.

"What are you doing, loser?" Zoe yelled, wiping the glop off the side of her neck. "We're on the same team!"

Zack couldn't help but giggle.

Just then, zombie Doris picked up a pan of goulash and heaved it over the barrier. A flying blob of ground meat and pasta sauce arced through the air and splattered Ozzie and Zack across their chests.

Okay, Zack thought. *Now it's on.*

Zack grabbed a tray of meatballs and started firing them at the undead lunch ladies. Doris caught one in the mouth and swallowed it whole. She retched, stumbling into the tables, and sputtered meat crumbs into the air, spraying Rice's face with half-chewed bits of beef.

Carol and Darla toppled over the second table, tearing ferociously through the tangle of upturned chairs. Zack grabbed his baseball bat from the floor next to the conked-out zombie janitor.

"Which way to the principal's office?" Ozzie shouted over the ruckus.

Zack paused, struggling to remember the blueprint of the school. Rice and Zoe were still gunning fistfuls of leftovers at each other while the zombified lunch ladies stomped toward them, clawing at the air. "Guys!" Zack called to them. "Quit it!"

Zoe and Rice stopped throwing food for a second and looked at each other. "Truce," Rice said, dropping his handful of spaghetti.

Zoe pretended to stop and then side-armed an oatmeal cookie like a Frisbee through Rice's face mask, whacking him on the nose. "Just kidding."

"*Glaargh! Hissssss.*" The lunch ladies lurched forward.

"Hurry up!" Ozzie shouted, and the others finally followed.

They ran back down the locker-lined corridor with Zack in the lead. The morning sun beamed through the window across from the door to the boys' locker room, lighting up the end of the hallway like a beacon.

"C'mon," Zack said. "I know a shortcut."

CHAPTER

They burst through the locker room door and scurried down the rows of gym lockers and long wooden benches, which were strewn with white towels blotched with pale green slime.

Zoe glanced to her left, looking into the boys' bathroom. "Whoa . . . you guys got some weird toilets."

"*Blarrgheckheckhlargle!*" a zombie croaked, and they spun to the right.

An agile eighth-grade zombie jumped out from the shower room in full wrestling regalia. Its headgear was partly askew over its crown, and a nubbly bump of cauliflowered flesh bulged out from under the ear protector.

Its spandex one-piece uniform was torn, revealing four parallel scrapes from a zombie clawmark. The wrestler zombie hopped and bobbed in an athletic stance while trying to lick its own ear.

"Tom?" Zoe asked, recognizing her classmate.

Zombie Tom lunged at Ozzie, grappling at his shoulders WWE style.

The zombie jockmeister reached for Ozzie's groin, angling for a body slam, but Ozzie lifted his leg and spun. Now he had the eighth-grade freak in a half-nelson sleeper hold. "Quick," Ozzie called to Rice. "Open the locker!" Rice flung open the metal door with a loud

clank. Zack grabbed the zombie's feet as Ozzie stuffed it inside and slammed the door.

"Good work, guys!" Zack slapped Rice and Ozzie on their shoulders.

"Hurry up, dorks!" Zoe yelled, depressing the metal push-bar at the exit. She opened the door, and they crept through the side entrance into the dark gymnasium. Zack led the way across the basketball court. The hardwood felt tacky, like the floor of a movie theater. Tipped-over refreshment tables littered the sidelines with smashed desserts and empty bowls of punch. Rice walked over to the mess and bent down. He picked up a lemon square from the floor and inspected it for a second.

"Ewww!" Zoe cried in revulsion. "He's eating off the floor!"

Rice gobbled down the yummy goody, swallowed happily and sighed. "They only make the good desserts for the parents."

"Rice, what are you doing?" Zack scolded. "There could've been zombie slime on that."

"I don't care, Zack," he responded. "Those lemon things are to die for."

"Shhhh!" Ozzie said. "Listen."

Just then, a red ball boinged out of the shadows and rolled to a stop at Zoe's feet. "Huh?"

A figure staggered out from underneath the bleachers and grabbed Rice by his book bag. It was their middle-aged, undead gym teacher, Mr. Ziggler, decked out in a green Adidas warm-up suit.

Rice tripped backward, crab-walking on the floor, as the zombie gym coach lurched toward him. "I'll run laps, Mr. Z.!" Rice pleaded. "I'll do my push-ups! Just leave me alone!"

In a flash, Zoe picked up the dodgeball and heaved it at the Ziggler zombie.

The bouncy ball spronged off its head. Unfazed, Mr. Ziggler roared, reaching down and swiping at his out-of-shape pupil.

"Aaaaaah!" Rice screamed.

Zack stepped up with his bat and swung, clubbing the capture-the-flag guru to the hardwood.

Rice took a deep breath, and Zack pulled his buddy off the floor.

"Uh, guys . . ." Zoe pointed behind them. An army of moms and dads, teachers and staff rose out of the stands and shambled onto the gym floor.

Their art teacher, Mr. Dickens, staggered side by side with Mrs. Thomas, the eighth-grade history teacher. Mr. Dickens's pink dress shirt was finger-painted red and black with zombie guts, like kindergarten art. Mrs. Thomas rasped, gurgled, and wheezed. Her arms waggled straight out in front of her face, sappy with purple goop.

Ozzie strode over to the pigeon-toed duo, brandishing his field hockey stick.

"Mrs T.'s about to be history," Rice quipped.

Ozzie swung the bludgeon low, one-handed, and swept the zombie teacher's feet right out from under it. He twirled the wooden cudgel like a baton and bopped Mrs. Thomas on the noggin. The reanimated corpse hit the floor with a crunchy double-*splat*.

Class dismissed.

"Run!" Ozzie ordered as the undead parents and faculty stormed the court.

Zack pulled the gym doors open, and they all stood at the top of the steps overlooking the lobby. The zombie-packed corridor resounded with wet, phlegmy moans.

"*Glargle snargle rhargh!*" Another wretched slew of zombie teachers gushed into the center of the lobby, hacking up goop.

"Stay here." Zack darted quickly back into the gym. The zombies shambled down the three-second lane.

Zack grabbed the metal bars on the two basketball racks, wheeled them onto the landing, and slid the shaft of a lacrosse stick through the door handles, sealing the other zombies inside the gym. "What are

those for?" Rice asked, taking a
practice swing with his field
hockey stick.

"Dodgeball . . . ," Zack
said, slapping the hard leather.

"Dude, you know I hate dodgeball."

"Don't worry, Johnston." Zoe picked up a ball, too.
"You won't get picked last . . . you're already on the
team." She spun the basketball on one finger.

"Head shots only, guys!" Ozzie
commanded, picking an And 1
rubber basketball off the
rack. He launched the rock
at Mr. Milovich, clobber-
ing him in the forehead.
The zombified guid-
ance counselor
dropped to the
lobby floor.

"Nice shot,
Oz!" Rice said,

giving props, and picked up a basketball of his own. The four of them
rifled ball after ball with remarkable aim, blasting the zombies in
their putrid noggins.

Suddenly the evil drama teacher,
Ms. Merriweather, pounced
up the steps, snatching
for Zack's feet. She
wore a frilly blouse,
covered in dreck and
slime, and weird jeans pulled up too high
above her waist.

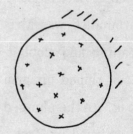

Zack grabbed another
ball and gunned it at the
drama zombie's pale, with-
ered face, blasting its temple.
SPLAMMO! The zombie teacher
dropped in a vile heap.

"Did we win yet?" Rice asked, panting to catch his
breath. He punted the basketball like a goalkeeper, too

tired to throw anymore. The ball ricocheted off the ceiling and nailed Mrs. Ledger, the fifth-grade homeroom teacher, on the top of its dome. Rice pointed at the zombie. "You're out!"

Suddenly, another drove of zombies shambled into the lobby from a side hall, like a video game blitz. They dribbled slimy snot strings, and knots of clotted pus dripped from their every quadrant.

"We're not winning, man!" Zack yelled.

Rice threw another lucky shot that bashed Vice Principal Liebner in the head. "Really?" He pumped his fist. "'Cuz it feels like I'm winning . . ."

Suddenly, a zombie hand tugged at Zack's shoulder from the side. He wheeled around. It was Mrs. Amorosi, the head librarian, groaning and slobbering at the top of the platform. Zack ripped his arm away, and the zombie stumbled back, but then lunged for him once more. A basketball whizzed by Zack's ear and caught the off-balance bookworm square in the face. *WHAM!* The she-zombie wobbled and fell backward down the stairs.

"There are too many of them!" Ozzie shouted over the ruckus.

Zack's belly filled with panic as more and more zombies rambled into the congested hallway of the school.

"No more dodgeball." Zoe pouted, pointing to the empty racks.

The gym doors rattled behind them. Grotesque hands and arms shot through the frosted glass windows, reaching around blindly just above their heads.

"We gotta get outta here!" Rice cried, ducking under the canopy of zombie appendages.

Zack bounded off the steps, skidding in a slick puddle of something gross. Zoe, Ozzie, and Rice raced down the stairs, ducking and dodging through a windmill of rotted arms and legs.

All of a sudden, Senora Gonzalez shoved her way past two of her zombified colleagues, groping wildly for Rice once again. She hurled herself forward, tackling him into the glass trophy case.

"*¡Arrozzzzzzz!*" she bleated.

"*¡No me gusta! ¡Por favor!*" Rice shouted.

The zombie's teeth made a dull clank as it gnawed at his face mask.

The crazed Spanish teacher would have bitten his face off if Rice had not been wearing his helmet. Zack grabbed a soccer trophy and clubbed the zombie in the side of the head.

"You okay, man?" He pulled Rice up out of the shattered trophy case.

"Think so," Rice said, brushing himself off as he

shot Senora Gonzalez a scornful look.

"She's really got it in for you today, huh?"

"*Blaarrgh!*" The Milovich zombie pulled itself off the floor and lashed out at the boys once again, but Zack hopped back and socked it with a swift swing of his bat.

"You didn't see my parents, did you?" Rice asked.

"Not yet, buddy. Not yet."

"Come on, guys!" Zoe shouted, waving her arm next to Ozzie in a nearby doorway.

They sprinted through the middle school–turned–zombie madhouse until they came to a vacant corridor.

Or so they thought.

CHAPTER 9

A rowdy pack of undead adults raged at the end of the hall. The zombies thrashed at the walls, tearing the posted bulletins and student art-work to the floor. They flailed their disjointed limbs against the lockers. *Whap! Bang! Clang!*

Zack, Rice, and Zoe tugged on all the doors, look-ing for an escape, but the classrooms were locked. All except for one. It was Mr. Budington's first-period science class. Zack shooed everyone inside and shut the door quietly, locking the knob. Everybody caught their breath.

"That was close," Zoe huffed.

"It's not over yet." Ozzie put his ear to the door. "They're coming."

"Okay . . . okay, we need a plan." Zack scratched his head. "Rice, what's the plan?"

"I don't know. Ozzie, what do we do?" Rice asked.

"Well," Ozzie thought out loud. "My sensei taught me all sorts of combat strategies. . . ."

Welcome back to The Life and Times of Oswald Briggs, Zack thought.

Ozzie continued. "Have you ever heard of the 'Lure and Destroy' maneuver?"

"No, but it sounds awesome," Rice replied.

"Basically, it means we have to set a trap or cause some kind of diversion and then escape when the enemy's distracted."

"Wouldn't that just be called 'Lure and Escape'?" Zack asked.

Ozzie just stared at him.

"What are we supposed to distract the zombies with?" Zoe asked.

Rice marched across the science lab. A glass display

jar glimmered on the sunlit windowsill. It was Mr. Budington's human brain specimen. Rice picked up the jar and carried it over to the teacher's desk. The brain was a squiggly mound of pruned tissue, floating in the nasty yellow water.

"Rice, what are you doing with that?" Zoe demanded.

"Don't you know what this is?" Rice asked solemnly.

"That creepy Meredith Jenkins girl told me it's Mr. B.'s *actual* brain." Zoe cringed. "Ewww."

"That brain's not even real," Zack scoffed.

"Oh, it's real all right." Rice unscrewed the lid and reached into the jar. "I've always wanted to touch it."

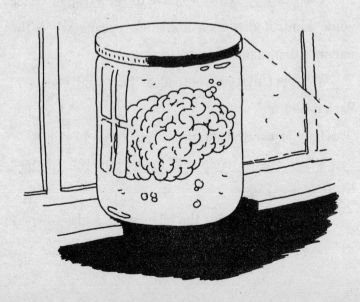

He pulled out the brain bare-handed and plopped it on the desktop. "The smartest brain the world has ever known." Rice poked at it with a stray no. 2 pencil. "Albert Einstein."

"Shut it, Rice!" Zoe pinched her nose as the thick formaldehyde fumes filled the classroom.

"Rice, seriously." Zack groaned. "Put that thing away."

"Zack, seriously, no," he retorted.

"Why not?"

Rice smiled, the hunk of brain-meat resting on his upturned palm. "Because this is the bait."

BAM! BAM! The whole wall shook, and they all whipped around.

Zack ran over to the door and peered out the little cross-hatched window. It was Mr. Budington.

And he wanted his brain back.

On the other side of the door, the zombie teacher banged violently, attracting more zombies with every thump.

Rice grabbed a piece of chalk and quickly scrawled PROFFESER RICE on the blackboard. Spelling had never

been his strong suit. He paced self-importantly at the head of the class, hands clasped behind his back, like a brooding college professor. "Please." He gestured to Zack, Zoe, and Ozzie to have a seat in the front row.

"Let me ask you one question: What do zombies love more than anything?" Professor Rice paused for a response, stroking an imaginary beard.

"Snorting?" Zack said from the front row.

"Moaning?" Ozzie guessed from the desk next to him.

"I liked the ripping-people's-faces-off part," Zoe said. "I mean, when I was a zombie."

"Brains, you guys!" Rice said, disappointed. "Now let me ask you another question. Why do you think the zombies always appear out of nowhere, even when we're being quiet?"

"Because they're everywhere?" Zoe said.

"That's true, Ms. Clarke, but no. . . . It's probably because the zombies have extrasensory receptors to home in on our brains."

"You mean, like, the virus uses the dead brains to hunt for other brains?" Zack asked.

"Precisely what I was thinking, Mr. Clarke." Rice nodded. "Gold star for you."

"So what's your brilliant plan, then?" Zoe asked brattily. "There's, like, fifty thousand of those yuck-mongrels out there, and all you have is one puny brain."

Mr. Budington thumped angrily outside in the hall-way. "*Braaaaiins!*" he bellowed.

"That's why we need something to cut it with," Rice explained, ignoring the angry, undead teacher.

"This'll work. . . ." Ozzie whipped out his sur-vival knife from a green plastic sheath fastened to his utility belt.

Rice took the knife, grinning. He touched the sharp blade to the meaty brain squiggles. Everyone groaned as Rice cut the brain into cross sections as if he were slicing a loaf of bread. The steel squished and squeaked through the rubbery specimen.

"I can't watch this." Zoe clutched her stomach and turned away.

Mr. Budington howled and groaned, banging on the door.

Twinkles licked a slice of brain. Zack and Zoe recoiled with disgust.

"Looks like he's still got a little zombie left in him." Ozzie chuckled as Rice finished carving the brain slabs.

"Now, for step two," Rice said. "Gimme a hand, Oz."

Rice and Ozzie pushed the teacher's desk against the wall, and Ozzie boosted Rice up so he could reach the top of the little window over the door.

"Suppertime!" Rice called down from his perch, opening the window. As he dangled the brain slices over Mr. Budington's head, the pounding on the door stopped. Rice then threw the cross sections Frisbee-style down the hallway. "Fetch!" The little brain patties smacked and slid across the linoleum floor. Dinner was served.

Zoe opened the door and watched as the zombies flocked to the cannibal's meatloaf at the other end of the hall. Zack could hear the squish and slurp of chewed brain.

Om nom nom. Nom. Nom. Nom. Nom.

Undetected by the feasting ghouls, Zack, Zoe, Rice, Ozzie, and Twinkles slipped out and finally made a break for the principal's office.

CHAPTER 11

Standing outside the office, Zack knocked lightly on the locked door. They waited in the uncertain silence. "Mom, are you in there?" he called out in a raspy whisper.

"Zack?" A muffled voice responded through the wood. The door opened an inch. Mrs. Clarke peeked one eye out through the crack and sighed. "Oh, thank goodness." She swung the door completely open, hustling them inside the principal's office.

Zack hugged his mother tightly around her waist. She clutched his head to her chest.

"Hi, Mrs. Clarke." Rice waved sheepishly.

"Hello, Johnston," she replied. Like mother, like daughter.

"Have you guys seen my parents around?"

"Sorry, honey. It got so crazy, we don't know if anyone escaped."

Rice bit his fingernail, starting to look worried.

"Where's Dad?" Zack asked.

"I'm up!" Mr. Clarke groaned, peering over the desktop. Zack's dad rose from the floor slowly, limping, with a big gash on his knee. Zack hugged his father.

"Hello, Rice," Mr. Clarke grumbled. "Who's this guy?"

Ozzie looked up from polishing the fermented brain residue off his survival knife. "Oswald Briggs, sir," he said. "Nice to meet you."

Zoe snagged a seat in Principal Lynch's whirly-chair and put her feet on the desk, with her hands behind her helmet. "Hey, Dad," she said. "Your leg isn't looking so great."

"Zoe?" Mrs. Clarke asked with surprise. "Is that you?"

"Hello, Mother."

"I didn't even know that was you under there," she

said. "Take off the helmet."

"Sorry," Zoe said. "It's for your own protection."

"Don't be silly. Take it off."

"You asked for it." Zoe removed the headgear.

Mrs. Clarke shrieked at the sight of her daughter's sore-freckled face. Zoe started to cry. "It's okay, sweetie, it's okay . . . ," Mrs. Clarke comforted her. She clutched Zoe tightly and stroked her stringy hair. "Your father and I know a wonderful plastic surgeon."

"Hey, honey—we can worry about our daughter's face some other time." Mr. Clarke turned the principal's computer around on the desk for everyone to see. The Web browser was open to YouTube with HOSTAGE MAKEOVER paused on the screen. Zack's face was being smeared by three different lipsticks at once. "You've got some explaining to do, young lady."

"It's true," Mrs. Clarke said, holding Zoe's shoulders. "Getting called into the principal's office during parent-teacher night does not a happy parental unit make."

Rice nudged Zack. "Why's your mom talking like Yoda?"

"Whatever," Zoe said, nibbling at her nails, her face

a bored mask of whateverness.

Zack's parents glowered at their firstborn child. Rice looked at something interesting on the ceiling and whistled a nervous tune. Ozzie glanced out the window, scanning the schoolyard for zombie threats. Zack waited for justice to be served.

"I think we need to call a family meeting," Mrs. Clarke suggested.

"Right now?" Zack and Zoe whined at the same time.

"Look . . ." Ozzie stepped in. "Mr. Clarke, Mrs.

Clarke, you two seem like swell parents and all, but as I'm sure you know, this place is crawling with zombies who want to eat us, and we should really get moving while we have the chance."

"Ummm . . ." Rice gestured at their only exit. "There goes our chance."

Everyone turned toward the office door.

Mr. Clarke said a bad word, which was bleeped out by Mrs. Clarke's scream.

Principal Lynch loomed in the doorframe, casting a huge zombie shadow across the floor. The big man wore the grin of a hungry predator that had just spotted its next meal. Zombie Lynch bellowed and yowled.

"Ahhh!" Zoe tipped back too far in the whirly chair, falling backward behind the desk.

The zombie's face was wet and clammy like a piece of deli ham. A tree of blue veins throbbed in its forehead.

Ozzie whirled his field hockey stick and ran at the superintendent of ghouls. He bounded forward with a flying side kick.

The zombie principal swatted Ozzie to the floor with

a single swipe of its gargantuan arm. Ozzie whacked his head against the edge of a file cabinet and slumped down, motionless.

I told him to wear a helmet, Zack thought.

Zombie Lynch limped forward, lumbering, a rope of gray, tangled snot swinging from its walrus-like mustache.

"Ready, Rice?" Zack looked at his buddy, and together, they charged.

Principal Lynch swung an arm again, backhanding the boys, which sent them both flying straight through the secretary's cubicle.

Zack's father hobbled forward, swaying like a wounded boxer. Apparently, the monster Lynch wanted to pick on someone its own size, or the next closest thing to it. The zombified principal lunged at Mr. Clarke, wrapping him up in its huge, bulky arms. The two grown men toppled to the floor.

Mr. Clarke fell flat on his back, underneath the massive zombie freak.

Then, just as the zombie principal was about to

clamp its filthy maw onto Zack's dad's shoulder, a deafening screech pierced the air. Rice was pressing the little squeaker button on the megaphone, and the zombie brute whipped its head around in the direction of the high-pitched noise.

Ozzie shot up, wielding the field hockey stick. He took two quick steps and swung like a pro slugger, smashing the sleek wooden cudgel into the soft temple of the zombified principal. The stick cracked in half. The zombie's spine went weak, and its head flopped to one side. A pus-like glob of cranial brain mucus spewed forth from the principal's puke-white ear as the headmaster ghoul dropped to the floor.

The contaminated blob landed directly on Mr. Clarke's wounded knee.

"Oh, it stings!" Zack's dad cried, clutching his thigh.

"Dad!" Zack shouted.

"Ewww . . ." Zoe squealed at the icky brain goo seeping into her father's leg. "So grody." She gave a little shudder.

"Do something!" Mrs. Clarke yelled, scurrying

over to her husband. She knelt down next to Mr. Clarke and blotted the slime-filled gash with her shawl.

"Stop, Mom," Zack said. "You're just smearing it in."

"Is that bad?" she asked.

"I don't know—is that bad?" Zack asked Rice.

"I mean, he wasn't bitten. You said the only way to be turned into a zombie is to be bitten by a zombie, right?"

Mr. Clarke howled louder. "That hurts!"

"Yeah, but . . ." Rice cleared his throat. "That was before we knew about BurgerDog."

"So what are you saying?" Zack asked. "My dad's gonna turn into a zombie?"

"It's gonna be okay, man." Ozzie put a comforting hand on Zack's shoulder.

Zack didn't respond, remembering the zombie colonel and thinking about how much he wanted his dad to stay his dad.

Rice pointed to Mr. Clarke's leg and made a dubious face. Blue swollen veins squiggled out from the infected flesh wound, spreading the zombie virus up the thigh and down the shin.

Ozzie squeezed past Zack and Rice. "How're you doing, Mr. Clarke?"

"How does it look like I'm doing?"

Ozzie pulled out his survival knife. "Listen, sir. I

know this isn't ideal, but if we act now, we can amputate the leg about midthigh before it spreads up any higher."

The shiny blade caught some light and sparkled in Ozzie's hand.

"Zack?" Mr. Clarke said, his eyes bugging out. "You keep this little psychopath away from me and I'll buy you anything you want."

Ozzie crouched down and examined the viral infection, scraping at it gently with the side of the knife. "We gotta get rid of this leg pronto."

"Zack . . ." Mr. Clarke looked up desperately at his only son. "Anything."

"Can I have Zoe's room?"

"Sure." He nodded.

"Hey!" Zoe shouted.

"Ozzie." Zack put his hand on Ozzie's shoulder. "I'm gonna go get some stuff from the nurse's office. Can you wait to cut my dad's leg off till I get back?"

"He's your dad." Ozzie shrugged. "Do what you want with him."

"I'll be right back," Zack said, and hustled out of the room.

"You're not supposed to say that, you know . . . ," Rice called after him.

CHAPTER 12

Zack bolted down the moaning hallway and barged into the nurse's office. He whipped open the supply cabinet and swiped some gauze and bandages, then snatched a bottle of peroxide. He closed the mirrored cupboard, catching a glimpse of his own reflection . . . and the reflection of someone behind him.

Or rather, some*thing.*

It was Ms. Nancy, the school nurse, plucking things out of her hair and nibbling at her fingertips. Her head turned slowly toward Zack, and the former Nurse Nancy revealed the other side of its face. One eye was encrusted with curdled skin, and the cheek was missing, exposing her gums and jaw muscles.

Zack spun around, ready to battle the zombie nurse. But it just kept muttering gibberish, digging at its grub-infested scalp for little snacks. Zack cocked a wary eyebrow and slammed the door, racing back down the corridor with the first-aid supplies.

Back at the principal's office, Zack closed the door softly behind him. "How's he doing?" he asked.

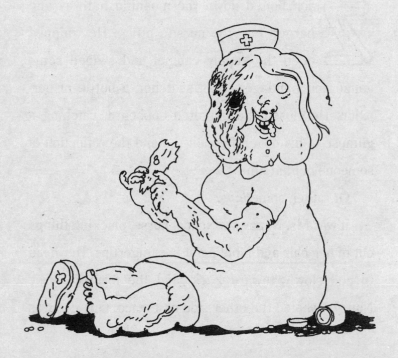

"Not good," Zoe replied. For the first time all night, she looked scared, too. Her eyes teared up as she looked down at their father. "Daddy?"

Mr. Clarke was sickly pale and sweating profusely. Mrs. Clarke was holding the back of his head. Zack raced over to his father's side and twisted the cap off the peroxide bottle. Mr. Clarke lifted his head slightly and smiled weakly at his son. Zack smiled back. "It's gonna be okay, Dad. I promise." Mr. Clarke's head dropped to the floor and he went limp.

Zack's stomach dropped.

Rice came over and put his arm around Zack's shoulders. "There was nothing we could've done."

"We coulda lopped it off . . . ," Ozzie said gruffly.

"Shut up, Ozzie!" Zack poured the hydrogen peroxide on the infected gash, and his dad's knee sizzled with white fizz.

"That's not gonna work, Zack," said Zoe.

"Yes, it will!" Zack started to choke up, his eyes shimmery with tears. "Come on, Dad. Come on . . . come on . . ."

Zack's eyes prickled with teardrops. He was so

tired, it hurt. All he wanted was to wake up and discover it was all a bad dream. And to have his dad back
again. And their house. And his stupid little life.

"Brouharghah!" Mr. Clarke thrashed to a seated position and latched on to Mrs. Clarke's calf. She howled in
pain as her undead husband ripped into her flesh like
it was a barbecued turkey leg. Zack's mom fell to the
ground, screaming in pain.

Zack and Zoe pulled Mr. Clarke off their mother and threw their zombie dad to the ground. Ozzie raised the aluminum bat to clobber Zack's own pops, but Zack grabbed Ozzie by the forearm.

"I'll do it," he said. Zack took the bat and wiped his eyes, before bopping his zombie dad on the head.

Rice took off his lacrosse helmet, fit it over Mr. Clarke's unconscious noggin, and fed him a handful of ginkgo biloba pills. "So he won't wake up."

"We need Madison," Zack moaned.

"What does Madison have to do with anything?" Mrs. Clarke asked. She grimaced, gripping the zombie bite.

"Zoe used to be a zombie until Madison changed her back. Long story," Zack explained.

"Great, let's go get her," Mrs. Clarke said hopefully. "Where is she?"

"Washington, D.C.," Ozzie said.

"Washington?"

Suddenly, the interior office windows shook. Outside in the hallway, the zombified faculty battered the glass with their heads and fists.

Here we go again, Zack thought. He hopped onto the oak credenza and hoisted up the blinds to the outer windows. The parking lot was right across the narrow side lawn.

Crash! Bang!

Zack looked over his shoulder. The hallway window was now a hideous mural of zombie teachers' facial features smashed into deranged expressions against the rattling glass.

"How do you open these things?" Zack cried frantically. The window wouldn't budge.

"Just smash it, man!" Ozzie shouted.

Zack twisted into a batter's stance and swung as hard as he could. The window shattered into pieces on the floor.

Behind them, the interior window looked like thin ice cracking over a frozen pond. *CRASH!* A zombie's fist smashed through the glass. Its flesh peeled back, revealing white meat and bone.

"Come on!" Zack called. "Hurry!" He bashed the

remaining glass shards off the outside window frame, and Twinkles leaped off the ledge, landing safely in a bush.

Zoe jumped out next and helped her mother maneuver her chomped leg gingerly over the windowsill.

Then Zack, Rice, and Ozzie lifted Mr. Clarke up and heaved him helmet-first through the window, away from the hollow yowls of the zombified parents and faculty. The boys hopped out last.

Safe outside, Mrs. Clarke hunched over, gasping.

"Put this on, Mom." Zack held out his football helmet. "I know it's annoying, but it's so you won't bite us."

"I'm not going to bite you, honey. . . ." Mrs. Clarke looked up. Her face began to mutate with swollen rot. "I'm gonna eat your brains!"

Mrs. Clarke's neck twisted grotesquely, rotating completely around. Zack jumped back and circled his reanimated mother as she let out a wretched groan. He capped the helmet over her backward head.

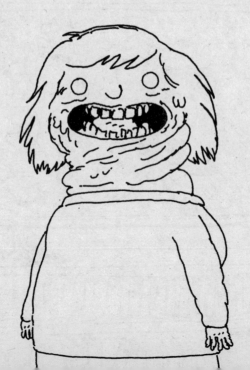

Zoe helped Zack lug their moaning zombie mom into the parking lot. Rice and Ozzie followed, dragging Mr. Clarke along the sun-baked cement. As they dragged him over a speed bump, his keys clatter-jangled on the pavement, and Rice bent down to retrieve them.

"Dad works at the bank . . . ," Zack mused. Rice handed him the keys.

"You wanna rob it?" Zoe asked in perfect seriousness. "Let's rizz-ole."

"No," Zack said, eyeing their zombified parents. "I wanna make a deposit."

"That's nice," Zoe said, snatching the keychain from her brother. "But I'm driving."

CHAPTER 13

Main Street was trashed and desolate, strewn with plastic bags and debris. Broken-down cars lined both sides of the uninhabited avenue, and most of the shops and restaurants had been demolished during the zombie attack. Goopy trails of zombie sludge baked on the blacktop. The junk-ridden road reeked of hot garbage. Amazingly, there were a few stores left untouched, like the lone homes remaining in the aftermath of a tornado.

Zoe slammed the brakes, and they lunged to a stop in front of their father's local branch of Phoenix Savings and Loan.

"All in favor of Zoe never driving again say 'aye,'"

Ozzie said, still clutching the grab handle after their herky-jerky joyride through the Arizona suburb.

"Look!" Zoe pointed out the windshield.

Just down the street a majestic, tan-checkered giraffe nibbled at a treetop.

It must have escaped from the zoo, Zack thought.

The eighteen-foot beast swung its long neck toward the car, licking its chops. The giraffe stared at them for a peaceful second and walked away, whapping its black tail tamely.

The four of them hopped out from the Clarkes' minivan, lifted the back door, and pulled Mr. and Mrs. Clarke across the sidewalk to the front of the bank. Zack swiped his father's debit card, and the glass door opened.

Inside the sweltering ATM

foyer, Zack tried the next set of doors, but they were locked. He riffled through the keychain until he found the right key, and then they dragged the zombified parental units into the main lobby.

Behind the tellers' counter, they stood before a giant steel door with a big metal wheel and a keypad. Zack found the key he'd seen his dad use before and stuck it in the lock. The keypad lit up: ENTER PASSCODE.

Zack ducked his head under the cashier's post and looked up at the underside of the countertop for the number. "Dad has a terrible memory," he explained.

"Maybe you should give him some ginkgo," Rice said, and nudged Ozzie.

Zack punched in the numeric code on the touch pad, and the dead bolt clunked. He spun the wheel counterclockwise, and the thick iron door eased open. The walls were shelved with blocks of crisp cash wrapped in plastic.

"Yo," Rice said. "We're loaded!"

"No, we're not," Zack said. He grabbed his father under the arms and dragged his catatonic pops inside the big safe. Zoe followed, dragging their snaggle-toothed mother. Mrs. Clarke snapped and snarled loudly behind the face mask of the football helmet.

"Zack . . ." Zoe looked down at their parents. "Are they going to be okay?"

"I hope so, Zoe. I really hope so."

"At least we know Madison will give us first dibs on the antelope. I'm her besty."

Zack turned to his undead mother. "We-yer go-ing to come back for you. . . ." He spoke in slow, broken syllables, trying to make her understand.

"She's not listening to you, dude. Maybe this will help." Rice unloaded a half bottle of ginkgo biloba from his backpack. He tossed some pills into Mrs. Clarke's mouth, and she choked them down. "Nighty-night, Mrs. Clarke," he said softly.

"You guys almost ready?" Ozzie asked.

"Almost." Zoe snatched her mother's purse, ran through the lobby of the bank, and sat down behind Mr. Clarke's desk.

"What do you need that for?" Rice asked.

"That's for me to know and you to find out," Zoe said, pulling out a makeup case. The boys watched her flip open the compact and look nervously in the little square mirror. She turned away and began her post-zombie emergency makeover.

"Zoe, do you have to do that now?" Zack asked his sister.

"Yup."

Rice and Ozzie filed out of the vault, and Zack cast

one final look at his zombie parents. Mrs. Clarke snarled and hissed. "Don't worry. We'll come back," he promised her before clicking the bank vault locked. Zack stood in shock, leaning with his back against the door. He was running out of ideas.

Zoe spun around in the desk chair. "Ta-dah!" Her face was painted up like she was a seven-year-old beauty pageant contestant. She looked like a finalist in the World's Grossest Sister competition.

"Looking good, Zoe . . . ," Rice said. "But does your face still hurt?"

"Not really," she said, slathering her cheekbones with another layer of beige gunk.

"Well, it's killing us!" Ozzie shouted. He and Rice laughed and bumped fists.

"Will you three quit screwing around?" Zack said. "Don't you realize that without Madison, our parents are goners? That everyone's a goner?"

"It's true," Rice said, his shoulders slumping. "We don't know anything about the zombie life span or the antidote time frame or the recombinant vectors for cross-immunization. . . ."

"We need Madison," Ozzie and Zack thought aloud.

"If we only had a plane," said Ozzie, "we could get to Washington in no time."

Rice's mouth dropped open. "You know how to fly?"

"Of course I do," Ozzie answered.

Zack rolled his eyes. *Of course he does.*

CHAPTER

A short while later, Mr. Clarke's minivan slowed to a stop next to the barbed-wire fence surrounding the runway of Phoenix's International Airport. Zoe, Rice, Ozzie, and Zack hopped out, and Zack stretched his legs in the hot morning sun.

It felt good.

"You really know how to fly one of those?" Zack asked Ozzie, peering at the big commercial jets parked on the other side of the fence.

"Relax, Zack." Ozzie stuck one foot onto the metal mesh and pulled himself up with both hands. "I've had my pilot's license since I was, like, ten years old." Ozzie scaled up the tall fence easily, straddling the barbed wire at the top.

Rice nudged Zack. "I can't do that," he whispered. "Can you do that?"

"I don't think so, man," Zack said, looking up at the sharp spiral wire.

Ozzie dropped down on the other side of the tall barrier. "All right now, Zoe. Throw Twinkles to me. But make sure you throw him high enough, cuz . . ."

"No prob, Bob." Zoe turned her back to the security fence and arched her neck backward so she was looking upside down through the fence. "Ready?" She took a wide stance and cradled the puppy in the space between her knees. Twinkles flattened his ears, boggle-eyed with fear.

"Zoe," Zack said. "Don't even think about it."

His sister smiled her sinister smile.

"Zoe, don't!" Zack commanded.

She lobbed the little Boggle skyward.

"Yip, yip, yip!" Twinkles bow-wow-wowed over the high, treacherous fence. Ozzie caught the yelping pooch on the other side, and Twinkles hopped safely to the ground.

"Ladies first," Zoe said, pushing past the boys. She shot up the fence next and paused at the top, looking down at Zack and Rice.

"Are you doofuses coming or what?" Zoe began to scale down the opposite side. "Or is it 'doofi'? Because of, like, 'cactuses,' which is actually 'cacti' . . ." She found her footing back on solid ground. "You know what I mean, though— right, doofi?"

"How did she do that?" Rice asked. "She's like a freakin' acrobat."

Zack tried to climb up the fence next. It didn't go very well. He dropped down. It went from bad to pathetic when Rice tried next, failing miserably.

"Sorry, guys." Ozzie shrugged. "It looks like you two are gonna have to go through the airport. We'll get the plane and meet you at the boarding gates at the far end of the terminal."

"You're going to leave us?" Rice asked nervously.

"We can't risk getting bitten just because you guys are out of shape," Zoe explained.

"Plus, I'm the only one who knows how to fly," Ozzie added.

"He's right, Zack," said Rice.

"Don't worry, we'll be there," Zack called after Ozzie and Zoe.

"Check you on the flip side, turd brains," Zoe said, and frolicked off after Ozzie.

Twinkles barked and made a sad puppy face at Zack through the fence.

"Go on." He shooed the little dog away with his hand. "You can't come with us. Uncle Ozzie will take care of you. . . . Go!"

Twinkles ran away, then stopped and turned to look back.

"Go!" Zack commanded, and the confused little pup

chased after Zoe and Ozzie.

"Come on, Rice. Let's go," Zack said. And they raced to the front of the airport terminal.

Zack and Rice paused halfway through the doors, holding their weapons from the school's equipment room. The vast airport lobby bustled with the living dead. Dozens of airport personnel and frequent flyers tottered aimlessly around check-in counters slathered with guts. Stray body parts decorated the floor.

"Dude, we definitely need Ozzie . . . ," Rice said.

"Will you forget about your bromance for one second?" Zack said.

"What's that supposed to mean?"

"'He's right, Zack. . . . He's right, Zack . . . ,'" Zack said in a nagging voice. "You're always agreeing with him."

"What's your problem, dude?" Rice defended himself. "He's right a lot."

Just then, a nearby zombie tourist caught sight of them and bellowed.

The rest of the zombies turned. "Whatever." Zack sighed, gripping his bat. "Just run!"

They blasted into the mass of snarling beasts, bobbing and weaving their way toward the zigzagging security lane. The zombies swung their arms, but the boys batted them down like piñatas.

"Down there!" Zack pointed toward the lower level of the terminal. But a crew of zombie travelers trudged up the down escalator, slurping and slobbering.

More zombies poured in from the duty-free shop, cutting off their only other exit. Zack and Rice darted through the cordoned-off maze, racing to the security gate.

The zombies converged inward, knocking over the stanchions.

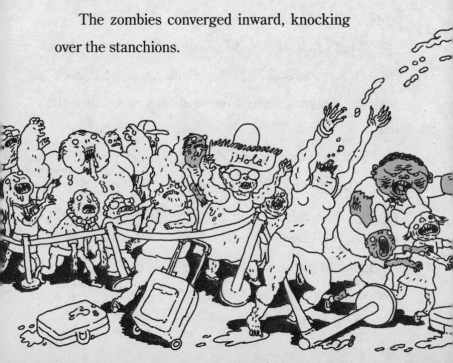

Zack and Rice were trapped, dead center, in a crazy cat's cradle of black vinyl straps tightening around their legs.

"Keep your knees up," Zack instructed, untangling his buddy from the tricky obstacle course. They high-stepped away from the zombie mosh pit toward the metal detectors.

"Hold it right there, kiddo!" An elderly airport security officer appeared out of nowhere. "Boarding pass and ID, please."

"You're not a zombie . . . ," Zack said, stunned. All around them, the undead staggered and swayed, but this old man was completely human. And completely oblivious to the zombie pandemonium coming their way.

"A what? What did you say?" The old man squinted at Zack. "Boarding pass and ID!" he repeated with more authority.

"Fine." Zack took out his Velcro wallet and showed the man his library card. The man nodded.

"Take off your shoes and remove all metallic items from your person."

"Sir, don't you see all these crazy zombies behind us?" Zack asked.

"Huh?" The old crackpot cupped his ear.

"Just let us through!" Rice yelled, looking over his shoulder at the mad free-for-all raging out of control behind them.

"I'm sure you're in a rush, but so are these good people." He motioned to the zombies, then handed the boys each a gray plastic bin. "Don't hold up the line, now."

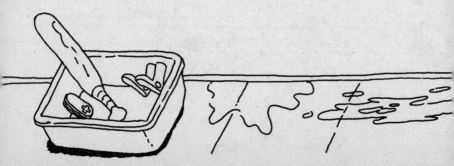

"But they're not even people!" Zack told him.

"Son, this isn't a joke. This is a matter of national security."

Zack put his sneakers, baseball bat, and Swiss army knife in the plastic bin, slid it into the carry-on scanner, and stepped through the metal detector.

"Arms out," the old man instructed. Zack groaned and put his arms out to the sides. The ancient security officer swiped the magnetic wand up and down his rib cage.

"*Sneerglsplargh . . . raah!*" The zombies reached out, grabbing and grunting, getting closer and closer with every moan.

Rice shuffled out of his shoes and tossed his backpack onto the conveyer belt. His zombie survival pack passed across the black-and-white X-ray monitor

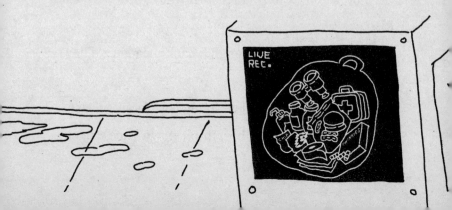

in negative. The screen showed the severed zombie fingertips twitching inside the Ziploc baggie, which also contained the diseased BurgerDog. A six-pack of snack-size potato chips lay crushed under the bottles of ginkgo biloba tablets. Crumpled homework assignments were crammed between an assortment of steel wool, duct tape, batteries, hand sanitizer, binoculars, a first aid kit, and a box of Twinkies.

"Mmm-hmmmmmm . . ." The old codger squinted at the X-ray as the zombies thrashed in the tangled lane behind them. "Please step through the metal detector, son."

Rice took one giant step through the magnetic doorway and stood still. *Beeep!*

The guard motioned Rice back through the detector. "Empty your pockets and come through again."

The zombies were a few feet away from devouring Rice.

"Sir, just let him through," Zack pleaded. "They're gonna rip his arms off!"

"I don't make the rules, sonny boy. Again, please."

The zombies were breathing down Rice's neck—

hot, pukey huffs of steam—as he frantically emptied his pockets of loose change and day-old Tater Tots. Behind him, a pale gray arm stretched out of its socket, reaching for Rice's shirt collar. The undead fingers were pruned and wrinkly, as though they had been too long in the shower.

In a flash, Rice ducked down and whacked the old security officer in the shin with his field hockey stick just as another zombie arm swiped overhead, humming through the air. Rice dove through the X-ray machine, and the old man howled, hopping on one leg and shaking his fist.

"Zack!" Rice cried from inside the machine.

Zack looked at the X-ray of Rice's skull. "Rice!"

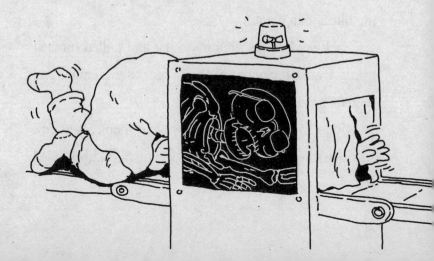

"Zack!" Rice's skeleton shouted hysterically from inside the machine. "I'm stuck!"

Zack reached in through the black rubber curtains and pulled Rice hard by the wrists. Just then, one of the zombies snatched Rice by the foot on the opposite side of the scanner.

"It's got me!" Rice screamed.

"Hold on!" Zack braced the soles of his feet against the machine's steel frame in a life-or-undeath tug-of-war. On a count of three, Zack yanked as hard as he could, and Rice came flying through the curtains, landing in a crumpled pile behind him. Zack skidded to get out of the way and fell with a *thud* on the hard smooth floor.

The zombie wriggled through the scanner, screaming like a mad demon.

Zack spotted his aluminum bat and pulled himself to his feet. He clobbered the screeching zombie, and then he rushed over to his pal.

"Rice? Dude?" Zack bent down and shook his buddy.

Rice's head flopped to one side, and his tongue lolled

out of his mouth. Zack put his ear to his friend's chest,
listening for a heartbeat.

"Rice, this isn't funny!"

But Rice wasn't moving. He was completely limp, just
lying there as the zombies raged behind the Plexiglas
security divider.

"Rice!"

CHAPTER  15

Gray plastic bins flew through the air as the knuckle-dragging mutants bottlenecked at the metal detectors, dragging the black vinyl straps and weighted metal stanchions like a zombie chain gang.

"Rice!" Zack shook his best friend as hard as he could.

Suddenly, Rice's eyes popped open. "Gotcha!" He smiled, jumped up, and dusted himself off, slinging his pack over one shoulder.

"Dude! You really need to stop doing that!" Zack yelled as they dashed for the boarding gates.

A short way down the wide, endless corridor, an

abandoned golf cart was parked in front of a BurgerDog X-press. The boys hopped in, and Zack sat behind the wheel.

"Thanks for saving me back there, man," said Rice.

"Sorry it wasn't Ozzie," Zack replied sarcastically.

"What's your problem?" Rice asked.

Zack sighed. "You know, it's just, like, you're my best friend and stuff, and then Ozzie shows up and it's, like . . ." Zack couldn't bring himself to tell Rice about his sickening fear of dropping to number two on his best friend's speed dial.

All of a sudden, a huge pack of googly-eyed ghouls thrashed out of a bookstore, sending the twirly racks of postcards and bestsellers crashing to the slime-spackled linoleum. "Umm, Zack?" Rice interrupted. "Can we maybe talk about this later?" He pointed at the stagger-ing green-eyed monsters.

Zack pressed the GO pedal, and the cart took off under the BurgerDog GRAND OPENING banner that hung across the high ceiling. They zoomed through the ter-minal, toward the distant boarding gates and away from the gathering zombie swarm.

A few minutes later, they hopped off the cart and stared out the giant windows overlooking the runway. "Where are they?" Rice asked.

"I don't know, but they better get here soon," said Zack, looking back the way they came.

The zombies were marching up the shiny metal corridor, their jaw muscles tightening and flexing. Their veiny necks flared with pulsing blood vessels and tendons, and their mucus-fed throats expanded and contracted with regurgitated phlegm. They waggled their arms like a parade of sleepwalkers, and from a distance, it seemed that all they really wanted were hugs.

Then, through the window, Zack saw the hot blast of a jet engine, and a commercial airliner pulled into view. Ozzie saluted from the cockpit. Zoe and Twinkles sat in the copilot's seat. She waved "hello" to the boys with the puppy's paw.

"Quick!" Rice raced over and opened the door to the boarding tunnel.

Zack dashed for the open entrance, looking over

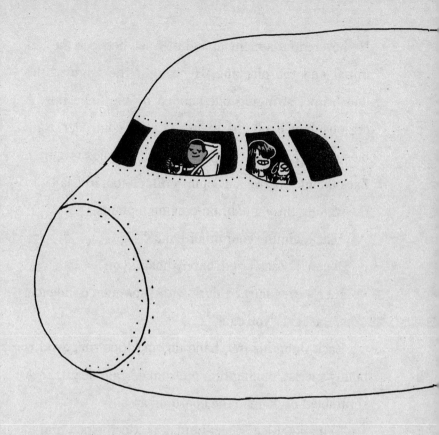

his shoulder at the dense mass of snargling fiends
behind them.

"Wait!" Rice screamed.

But it was too late.

There was no boarding tunnel, and Zack was already
treading air like Wile E. Coyote off the edge of a cliff.

He hovered for a moment and then fell between the terminal and the airplane. He caught the edge of the doorframe, swinging one-handed by his fingertips. A curious bunch of gnarly-eyed traffic controller zombies gathered below, gazing up with tongues wagging. Zack dangled above his doom: a fifteen-foot free fall into the waiting throng of brain-craving mutants.

"Zack, gimme your other hand!"

"I can't!" Zack cried, barely holding on.

Rice's eyes burned dark with supreme confidence. "Yes," he said, "you can!"

Zack flung his free hand up, and Rice snagged his buddy's wrist, pulling him up from certain death. Zack scrambled back up to the boarding area.

"Thanks, Rice," Zack huffed as Rice helped him to his feet. "Sorry about . . . you know."

"It's cool." Zack and Rice clasped each other's thumbs as if they were about to arm wrestle and hugged it out, patting each other firmly on the back.

But the tender moment was interrupted as Zack caught sight of the herd of gruesome zombie brutes getting even closer, growling and gnashing what remained of their teeth.

Snap! Snap!

"Grahrlgh!"

The zombified airport personnel waddled into the waiting area.

"That way!" Rice pointed across the boarding gate to a staircase. The boys raced away from the zombies and descended under a sign with arrows pointing the way: → GROUND TRANSPORTATION/→ BAGGAGE CLAIM.

The zombies chased clumsily after Zack and Rice, tumbling undead-over-heels down the flight of steps. The boys took off running through the lower level as the ghouls toppled into a hideous pile of snapped bones and decomposing skin behind them.

Straight ahead, the baggage carousel rotated cheerfully with a single unclaimed suitcase taking a ride on the merry-go-round.

Zack and Rice hopped on and squatted down, riding through the black curtains of the restricted area. Outside, they jumped off the carousel and dashed

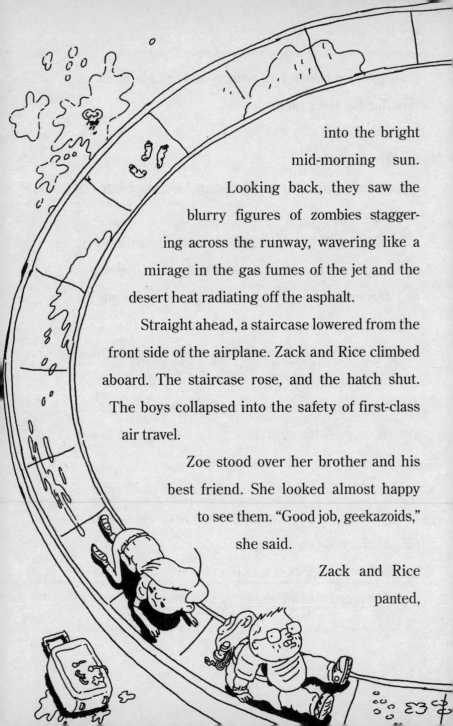

into the bright
mid-morning sun.
Looking back, they saw the
blurry figures of zombies staggering across the runway, wavering like a
mirage in the gas fumes of the jet and the
desert heat radiating off the asphalt.

Straight ahead, a staircase lowered from the
front side of the airplane. Zack and Rice climbed
aboard. The staircase rose, and the hatch shut.
The boys collapsed into the safety of first-class
air travel.

Zoe stood over her brother and his
best friend. She looked almost happy
to see them. "Good job, geekazoids,"
she said.

Zack and Rice
panted,

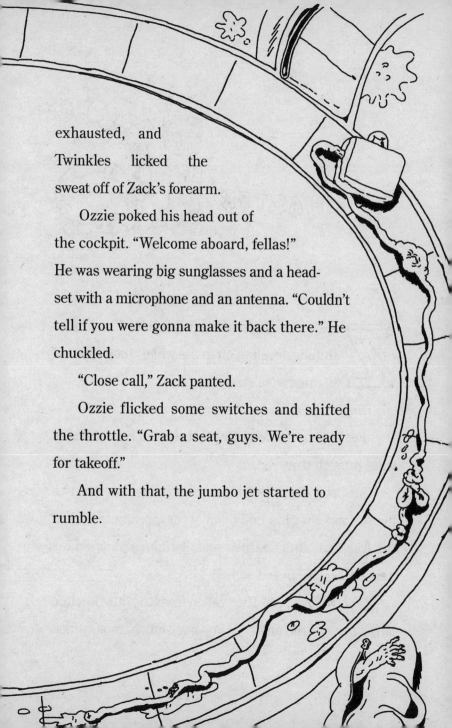

exhausted, and
Twinkles licked the
sweat off of Zack's forearm.

Ozzie poked his head out of
the cockpit. "Welcome aboard, fellas!"
He was wearing big sunglasses and a head-
set with a microphone and an antenna. "Couldn't
tell if you were gonna make it back there." He
chuckled.

"Close call," Zack panted.

Ozzie flicked some switches and shifted
the throttle. "Grab a seat, guys. We're ready
for takeoff."

And with that, the jumbo jet started to
rumble.

CHAPTER

Zack's ears popped as they cruised to higher altitude, leveling off in the white cloud vapor of an otherwise clear blue sky.

Ding!

"Feel free to move about the cabin." Their captain's voice projected overhead.

But Zack didn't feel like moving. He'd been awake for so long that his body was weary, ready to nap in the fresh-smelling leather seat. Twinkles plopped his head in Zack's lap and sighed.

"Okay, guys . . . ," Rice called from the little kitchen at the front of the plane. "They got Muncharoos, which

I think are like Cheetos, except with a kangaroo. From down undah, mate!" Rice did a weird Australian accent.

"What else?" Zoe asked.

"They also have chocolate-covered pretzels and . . . that might be it."

"Chocolate pretzels are yum." Zoe eagerly unlocked her tray-table.

"Bag of Muncharoos." Zack yawned groggily.

"What's the magic word?"

"Please," Zack added. Rice didn't move, waiting for Zoe.

"Now!" she insisted.

Rice grabbed the snacks, walked down the aisle, and dished out their orders before heading back to the kitchen area.

"I must say, dear brother, I'm much more fond of him when he's being our servant." Zoe laughed haughtily.

"*URGLE SPLARGH KAH!*" resounded from the pantry.

Rice screamed at the top of his lungs, and Zack shot up in his seat. A deranged zombie flight attendant had his buddy by the throat and was wringing Rice's neck.

Rice grabbed the mutant flight attendant by the throat, too, and they waltzed in place like a zombie slow dance, gagging away.

"What the—?" Zack bolted down the center aisle.

"Help!" Rice coughed and sputtered, locked in the two-way stranglehold.

The zombie flight attendant thrust its face forward

and snarled, spewing spittle as it frothed at the mouth like a rabid dog.

Rice's eyes were bloodshot, road-mapped with red veins. Zack lunged at the duo and grabbed the zombie by the hair, pulling back as hard as he could. The flight attendant let go of Rice's jugular and elbowed Zack in the nose. Zack fell back, and Rice broke free and toppled onto Zack.

The in-flight lunatic towered over the boys.

"Ahhhh!" Zack and Rice screamed together, holding each other like a couple at a horror movie.

All of a sudden, Zoe thumped down the aisle and threw a running haymaker with her right hand. *BAM!* She finished with a left uppercut. *POP!* The zombie dropped to the ground. Zoe rubbed her knuckles and shook her hand.

Rice massaged his throat and swallowed hard. "Tanx," he rasped.

"My pleasure, Ricee-poo." Zoe made a muscle and kissed it.

"C'mon, help me get rid of this thing." Zack picked

up the zombie by its ankles.

Zack and Zoe dragged the unconscious flight attendant to the back of the plane and tossed her in the coach bathroom.

Back in first class, they rode in silence. Zack sipped a soda, twitchy-eyed with sleep. He sunk his head into a pillow and drifted in his thoughts. He tried to settle into the throb of the jet, but whenever he closed his eyes, all he saw were floating zombie heads imprinted on the backs of his eyelids like a slideshow. He couldn't stop thinking about his mom and dad locked up in the bank vault. Zombified.

Zack pulled the shade down on the too-bright window. Rice appeared with a little red fleece blanket and tucked him in. And finally, Zack dozed off into a dreamless sleep.

Hours later, Zack woke up with a start. He opened his shade and peered outside. The bright morning sun had been replaced with a somber late afternoon light, even darker as they hurtled into a thick cloud. The inside of the airplane dimmed.

Zack looked to his right. Rice was snoring, fast asleep. Zoe was standing over him with a Sharpie, preparing to scribble something on his forehead.

All of a sudden, the cabin started to shake and rattle as if there were an earthquake in the sky.

"Ozzie!" Zoe shouted up to the cockpit. "What the heck are you doing?"

The jumbo jet started to corkscrew, and Rice woke up suddenly. "We're going down!" he shouted over the shriek of the juddering aircraft.

The FASTEN SEATBELT sign dinged on. Yellow oxygen masks dropped from the overhead bins. The snack cart flew out of the pantry, crashing down the aisle.

Twinkles bolted for Zack's lap, his ears flat against his head. Zack, Zoe, and Rice sat back stiffly in their seats.

Zoe turned to the boys. "Before we all die I—I . . . I just want to say that I'm sorry for always being so mean to the two of you. I love you, little bro! There, I said it."

"I love you, too, man!" Rice shouted to Zack.

"I love both you guys!" Zack closed his eyes and prayed they wouldn't crash.

No one said anything as the airplane dipped and swerved in the thunderstorm.

CRACK! BOOM!

"Okay, so now you guys apologize to me," Zoe said.

"For what?" Zack yelled over the rumbling chaos.

"For always being little nerd-mongers and provoking my meanness," she explained. A hollow rumble of thunder sounded. Lightning zapped outside the windows.

"Okay, okay," Rice said, terrified. "I'm sorry your face got all messed up."

Zoe crinkled her brow, dissatisfied. "It has to be something you did, dorkus."

The plane tilted suddenly, and everyone jerked.

"Fine!" Zack shouted. "When you busted through my bedroom door and tried to eat me, it felt kind of good to bash you over the head."

"Hey," Zoe said. "That's mean!" She looked over to Rice. "Well? What do you have to say for yourself?"

All of a sudden, the airplane leveled off.

"Well?" Zoe crossed her arms, still glaring at Rice.

The overhead lights came back on, and the cabin repressurized. Rice said nothing and stuck out his tongue.

Ozzie's voice came on over the loudspeaker. "Sorry, kids, just a little turbulence. There's a storm a-brewin'. It's gonna be a bumpy landing."

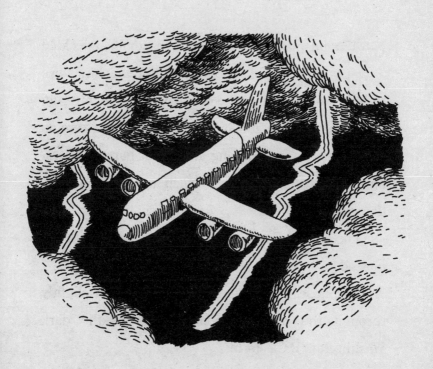

CHAPTER

The plane soared over the zombie-speckled parkway below. Zack caught the bird's-eye view through the oval window. The tottering masses looked like ants on the ground. There were no headlights. No cars driving at all. Just bursts of lightning illuminating the road, which was teeming with tiny ghouls.

The stormy East Coast city was crawling with the undead.

The nose of the jumbo jet tipped down slightly through the harsh, whipping wind of the dark Washington, D.C., storm.

Finally, the wheels of the plane touched down

on the rain-swept pavement of George Washington Memorial Parkway. The jet bounced back up, and Zack felt his stomach churn the way it did during a dip on a carnival ride. The entire cabin jolted. Zack, Rice, and Zoe bobbled around in their seats, rigid with fear. Zack hugged Twinkles securely in his arms. The puppy whimpered as the massive aircraft rocked to a stop.

Ozzie stepped out from the cockpit. "That went pretty well," he said confidently. "You guys ready to do this?" He grabbed the field hockey stick off the floor.

Zoe sat stiff in her seat, still clutching the armrests, eyes bulging. She didn't look ready at all.

"Chill, Zoe." Rice patted her on the head and grabbed his bag.

"Put Twinkles in there," Zack said. "I don't want him running away again."

"Good call, Zack Attack!" Rice pulled open the zipper.

"Not that pocket," Zack directed, eyeing Rice's specimens. "I don't want him eating any more BurgerDog, either. And don't call me Zack Attack."

Rice put Twinkles in the other pouch.

Zack glanced outside through the little window. "What time is it here?"

"Little after six," Ozzie said, slamming his elbow pad into the palm of his hand.

Ozzie popped the side hatch open, and they jumped onto the roadway. Huge, dark-green trees thrashed in the cold, wild wind. A vast plague of rain-drenched beasts shambled along the pavement. Zoe, Rice, Ozzie, and Zack shot past the zombie fiends and headed off the side of the road. They trampled down a hill through some tall, marshy grass and came to the edge of a great river, which looked ready to flood.

A flash of lightning lit up the sky.

Zoe shrieked—the zombies were sloshing and stumbling after them.

"Look." Ozzie pointed upstream.

Not too far away, a bridge spanned the river. "Run for it!" Zack shouted, and they booked it along the riverbank.

They sprinted away from the zombie mob to the other side of the river, stopping to catch their breath beneath two towering brass statues of colonists riding horseback. Ahead of them, the road forked around a massive white building surrounded by gigantic pillars.

"The White House . . . ," Rice said with awe in his voice.

"Actually, that's the Lincoln Memorial," Ozzie

corrected. "Haven't you guys ever been to Washington?"

"We live in Arizona, dude," Zack said.

"The White House isn't that much farther," Ozzie told them, and they took off around the back of the Lincoln Memorial into the tree-lined park.

"Hey," Rice called. "Wait up!"

Ozzie was running ahead of them, too fast. Zack hustled, trying to keep an eye on the one kid he did not want to lose track of.

Suddenly, a slime-smothered ghoul tottered out from behind a tree trunk. Zack dodged its flailing arm, trying to see through the downpour.

And just like that, Ozzie was gone.

"Ozzie!" Zoe yelled in the pelting rain.

Zack heard something howl like a wolf caught in a bear trap. *Ozzie?* Zack sprinted in the direction of the agonized noise. Up ahead, Ozzie was rolling in the mud, grasping his leg below the knee with both hands.

"*AHHHHHH!*" Ozzie wailed. His ankle was stuck in a scraggle of exposed tree roots. "My leg!"

"You okay, man?" Zack shouted, pulling Ozzie's foot

out of the hole. Ozzie yowled, gasping for breath, as the rainfall battered them.

"Ah, man," Rice said, catching up. "This is worse than when you forget to turn off injuries in *Madden*."

A zombie mailman staggered out from behind a nearby tree, slathered in slime. He bellowed a tortured moan, shambling toward them, going postal.

"We have to get Ozzie out of here," Zoe warned.

A lightning bolt split the sky, and Zack caught a snapshot of the scene around them. An endless rally of zombified citizens closed in on all sides. Mud-covered savages crisscrossed in the light and then disappeared

in a flash of shadow. The storm rumbled and popped with a furious burst of rain.

"To the Lincoln dude!" Zoe pointed through the trees to the memorial.

Zack and Zoe carried Ozzie across a roadway, away from the zombie onrush and up the short, wide steps between two gargantuan pillars. Under the shelter, they placed Ozzie on the cold marble and stared down at their wounded ninja soldier.

Ozzie pulled up his pant leg and grunted. It wasn't pretty. The shinbone was visibly cracked above his ankle, bulging under the skin.

"Dude," Rice said sorrowfully. "Your leg is busted!" He poked at it with his finger. Ozzie howled again.

"Rice, give me those binoculars," Zack ordered.

Rice dug around in his pack, plucked out the pair of binoculars, and handed them to Zack, who peered through the magnifying lenses.

"What do you see?" Ozzie asked, wincing, half in shock.

Zack saw the Reflecting Pool, tinted green, spilling

over with floating zombies, pruned and bloated. The tree-lined parkway was roiling with rain-soaked, brain-hungry fiends.

"A ton of zombies," Zack responded. "And, like, this giant spiky thing at the other end of a pond."

"Okay." Ozzie gasped. "That's the Washington Monument. You guys are gonna follow the pool and make a left at the big spike thing."

"What are you talking about 'you guys'?" Rice asked.

"Then go straight, all the way down, until you hit the White House," Ozzie went on, ignoring him.

"You're not coming?" asked Zoe.

"How?" Ozzie squeezed his broken leg. "I can't walk."

"Maybe we could just go real slow and the zombies wouldn't know we're not zombies." Rice staggered forward, his arms outstretched, doing a remarkably good zombie impersonation.

"I'm useless," Ozzie said. "Deadweight. Leave me here."

"No way, dude," Rice said. "We're not leaving you behind!"

The rain poured in buckets off the roof of the Lincoln Memorial. Zack paced back and forth nibbling his thumbnail.

"It's for the best," Ozzie said.

"I'm really good at three-legged races," Zoe blurted.

"Thanks, Zoe," Zack said. "But what does that have to do with anything?"

"Duh," Zoe retorted. "Just tie his bad leg to one of my good legs."

"Think you can do that, Ozzie?" Rice asked.

"It's worth a shot . . . ," Ozzie said, gnashing his teeth.

Zack and Rice helped Ozzie stand up and balance

on his good foot. Zoe stood directly next to him, putting her good leg against his bad one. Zack wrapped the three-legged racers with the last of their duct tape and chucked away the empty roll.

They stood now, the four of them on seven legs, under the watchful gaze of Abraham Lincoln, sitting on his oversized throne.

Zack looked out over the zombie-ridden capital of the

zombie-infested USA, and it dawned on him that this was not just about them anymore. It wasn't just about Madison, and it wasn't just about their moms or their dads or their puppies or their friends. A fist-sized knot tightened in his chest.

This was about everyone.

CHAPTER

I t was raining cats and BurgerDogs.

Zoe and Ozzie hobbled down the marble steps. Zack and Rice raised their weapons and moved slowly, flanking the three-legged racers. Ozzie shouted, "Ow!" with every other step they took as they made their way down to the Reflecting Pool.

Everything looked black and gray in the thunderstorm's dusk. Bloated bodies of puffy, waterlogged flesh floated facedown in the pelting rain. Sopping-wet zombies lurched out of the park's forest. A narrow zombie gauntlet formed between the treacherous woodland and the stone ledge of the long rectangular pool.

They moved toward the Washington Monument as quickly as Zoe and Ozzie could hobble. The rain beat fast with the pace of Zack's pulse as they stalked along through the zombie maelstrom.

"Zack, look out!" Rice called.

A sludge-drenched madman doddered out of the woods. Zack reeled around and swung his bat, clubbing the zombie with a mighty wallop. *KERSPLAT!* The ill-willed beast fell flat in the muck. Zack grunted.

Lightning lit the sky for a full two seconds. Up ahead, the pointed ivory monument cast a shadow across the green, like a dagger pointing toward their final

destination. The most famous house in America was no more than a few football fields away.

"The White House . . . ," Rice said again with the awestruck tone in his voice.

The landscape darkened, and thunder popped like a fireworks finale.

Zack gazed through the binoculars. Hundreds and hundreds of undead citizens prowled across the White House Rose Garden. Muck-covered politicians shambled in the flashing darkness. Senators plodded through the sludge side by side with homeless bag ladies, and evil-eyed children tottered beside escaped

zombie prisoners in orange jumpsuits.

The sewer grates off the curb were plugged with thick black gunk and debris, causing the roadway to flood. Insects and rats' tails coated the surface of the water—a real witch's brew of stink and filth. Hot dogs and eyeballs bobbed in the slow current of the contaminated moat they now had no choice but to cross.

"Can we do this?" Rice shouted over the rain's loud splatter.

"We're gonna have to, man!" Zack turned to Ozzie and his sister. "How are you guys doing?"

"He's a really bad partner," Zoe said. "But we'll be okay."

Zack hiked up his pant legs and gripped his bat firmly. Rice walked softly, carrying a big field hockey stick. Ozzie growled, wincing with every step Zoe took, as they waded across the street brimming with diseased slop.

A well-dressed gang of zombified politicos tottered in tattered sport coats across the South Lawn of the White House. A zombified congressman and a Senate page lurched toward them, waving their mutilated arms.

Shredded Oxford sleeves dangled from their elbows, dribbling ooze.

Rice clobbered the lowly intern, and Zack belted the politician in his legislative noggin.

Zoe trudged along through the puddles of muck, dragging Ozzie, as her brother and his buddy thumped and swatted through the undead madness. They were almost there.

"Come on!" Zack and Rice shot up some marble steps and waited for Zoe to drag Ozzie and his dead leg up, too.

"She better be in there," Zoe said, out of breath at the top. Ozzie pulled out his big knife and cut them loose. The three-legged race was over.

Zack lifted open a window and climbed over the sill, landing on the plush carpet of the interior. Rice tumbled through the window next, followed by Zoe. Ozzie limped inside, using the field hockey stick as a cane.

As they made their way up a staircase in the abandoned mansion, Zack paused midway, sniffing the air. "Do you smell that?"

Zoe breathed in deeply through her nose. "Uckh!"

she coughed. "Rice, was that you?"

"Sorry," said Rice. "I'm nervous." He waved his hand behind his rump.

"Man." Ozzie shook his head. "That's awful."

"Not him!" Zack groaned. "It smells like coffee up there."

He led the way to the second floor, twitching his nostrils like a bloodhound, as they followed the scent of fresh-brewed coffee to the door outside the Oval Office.

They entered the President's inner sanctum.

A Secret Service agent swung around to face Zack. He wore a black suit and sunglasses and carried a cardboard tray that held four cups of coffee. The man in black swept his coat away and reached for his hip like a Wild West gunslinger. His hand gripped the cold black metal of his firearm.

Panicked, Zack looked over his shoulder at Rice, Zoe, and Ozzie.

The sopping-wet trio looked bedraggled and frightening. Rice wheezed loudly. Ozzie wobbled, balancing on one foot, grimacing and snarling through the pain of his cracked leg bone. Streaks of makeup ran down Zoe's face, making her look like the Joker from *The Dark Knight.*

"Wait! We're not zombies!" Zack shouted.

"Coulda fooled me." The Secret Service dude sighed, and he took his hand off his holster. "Your friends blend right in."

"Where's Madison Miller?" Zack stepped forward.

"How do you know about her?" asked the agent. "She's classified information."

Zack sucked in a deep breath and exhaled slowly through his nose. He told the tale of ginkgo biloba and BurgerDog and Madison's immunity and Greg's unzombification into NotGreg. Of the colonel and his parents. Of the cross-country flight and their brushes with death.

There was a long pause. The man in black took a sip of coffee and wiped his eyes. Was he *crying*? Then he stuck out his hand. "Special Agent Gustafson."

"Zack Clarke, Zombie Chaser." Zack shook Agent Gustafson's hand.

Agent Gustafson walked over to a large portrait of George Washington hanging over the fireplace. "Come with me," he said, flicking the gold-leaf frame on the bottom of the painting. It flapped open like the hidden controls on a television set.

Agent Gustafson punched a series of numbers on the keypad. The portrait shook, and the fireplace lifted, revealing a dim, oak-paneled hallway lit by fancy light fixtures that looked like lanterns. The hall was furnished with antique end tables and built-in bookshelves. A thin Persian carpet ran the length of the passageway, and the walls were hung with famous-looking paintings.

The group followed Agent Gustafson to the dead end of the secret hall, where he stopped in front of a bookcase. Then he picked a thick, leather-bound volume off the shelf, took off his shades, and looked into the empty slot where the book had been. A blue laser scanned his eyeball, and the bookcase disappeared as it lowered into the floor and revealed a clear booth made of thick plastic.

"Get in." The man ushered them inside and pressed a button labeled z on the elevator panel.

Zack watched through the glass walls as the transparent booth dropped rapidly down, down, down. Zack looked at the secret service agent. Could he be trusted? He seemed okay, but if Zack had learned anything at all in the past twenty-four hours, it was that nothing was ever really what it seemed.

"Where are we going?" Zack asked Agent Gustafson.

The man didn't answer.

Bing!

Wherever it was, they had arrived.

CHAPTER 19

The glass wall of the phone-booth elevator opened, and they all stepped into a sterile metal passageway that looked like an oversized air vent. A set of hospital doors swung open automatically on their approach and they entered the top-secret laboratory located somewhere underneath the White House.

"Gustafson!" a voice boomed. "Where's my mother-lovin' coffee?"

A big man in a military uniform walked toward them from the back of the room.

"This is Brigadier General Munschauer, White House chief scientist."

"Who are they?" The general pointed at the kids.

"They're friends of the girl, sir."

"Where's Madison?" Zack demanded.

"Watch who you're talking to, hotshot. I haven't had my evening coffee yet." The general picked up a cup from the tray and took a sip. "*Kah!*" He savored the taste, sniffing the hot drink. "Your friend is quite a specimen. . . . How did you get here all the way from Phoenix?"

"Ozzie flew us," said Rice, gesturing to their wounded pilot.

"The boy's leg needs attention, sir," Agent Gustafson explained.

The general bent down on one knee and inspected Ozzie's fractured shin. He looked up at Agent Gustafson. "Take him to Room twenty-three. Tell them to reset the bone and cast him up." The special agent carted a wheelchair over to Ozzie, who plopped down in the seat and was rolled off down the hall.

"Follow me," the general said. He led Zack, Rice, and Zoe to a curtained-off section of the laboratory.

"Right now she's stable," General Munschauer said. "But she's lapsed into a metabolic retox and her B and T cells are severely depleted."

"Not possible," Zoe said. "Madison doesn't even eat BLTs. . . . She's a vegan."

"You're not really speakin' our language, sir," Zack explained.

"See for yourselves." The general pulled back the curtain.

They gathered around the gurney.

Madison had a plastic tube running up her nostrils and an IV tube stuck in her arm. Her skin was gray and wrinkly, and she took quick, shallow breaths. Suction cups were stuck to her forehead. Dangling tubes and plastic cylinders filled with variegated fluids hung around her face. Her eyes were shut, and a heart monitor beeped slowly with her pulse.

"Is she asleep?" Rice asked.

"Not exactly . . . ," General Munschauer replied dismally. "She's recuperating."

"She looks like ET at the end of *ET*," Zoe said, her voice quivering.

Zack turned to the general. "She's going to be okay, right?"

Munschauer cleared his throat. "We hope so. . . ."

Zoe petted her friend's head and whimpered, "You used to be so beautiful."

Just then, Rice's backpack started to rustle and growl. Twinkles barked. Rice unzipped his bag, and the tiny Boggle pup jumped out. Zack scooped him up, and Twinkles whined happily.

"Arf!"

The heart machine next to the stretcher beeped faster, and everyone turned toward the gurney.

Madison opened her eyes. "Twinkles?" she whispered meekly.

The puppy jumped from Zack's arms onto the stretcher. Twinkles licked Madison's face delicately.

"Hey, boy . . ." Madison coughed softly.

"You all should be extremely proud of your friend," the general told them. "Her courage is remarkable. She single-handedly unzombified the First Family, and because of her, a lot of important people are still human."

"Well, what about the second family . . . and the third . . . and the millionth?" Zack demanded. "A lot of people need her help—not just the 'important' ones."

"If Madison had known you weren't helping everybody, she'd never have let you use her up," Rice said.

All of a sudden, a tall woman with red hair opened the curtain. She wore a white lab coat with a name tag that read DR. DANA SCOTT, DISEASE & IMMUNOLOGY TASK FORCE. She pulled down a mint-green scrub mask from her face.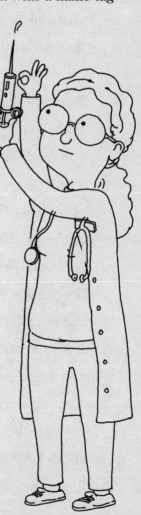

"Time for your shot." Dr. Scott squeezed past the kids, holding a large syringe. She squirted some liquid into the air and flicked the tip of the needle.

"I'll leave you to your business," General Munschauer told the doctor, and left.

"No more needles," Madison said wearily.

"This is just a B-twelve shot to help boost your immune system," she said kindly. She pinched

Madison's arm and depressed the plunger.

"What's the *B* stand for?" Rice queried.

"Vitamin B."

"Oh," he said. "I thought it was for 'biloba.'"

"Like ginkgo biloba?" Dr. Scott laughed. "Why?"

"Because that's, like, the whole reason she's the antidote."

"What are you talking about?"

"Yeah, and if you give ginkgo to zombies, it knocks them out and, like, slows the zombie virus or something. . . ."

"Slows down the virus, really . . . ?" Dr. Scott stared off into the lab, thinking out loud. "But without an original specimen, I can't produce a serum. . . ."

"Specimens?" Rice nudged Zack. "We've got mad specimens. . . ."

"If we just had a sample of the original virus, then I might be able to generate a viable base serum to mass produce the antidote . . . ," she went on, still talking to herself.

Rice wriggled out of the shoulder straps and reached into his pack. He held up the plastic bag with the zombified fingertips still twitching around inside. Rice then opened the Ziploc baggie and dumped out the revolting day-old zombie burger. The processed mystery meat pulsated as if it were alive.

The stench was gut-wrenching. Zack's nose crinkled. Dr. Scott's eyes widened with excitement. Twinkles's snout twitched wildly, catching a whiff of the rank hot-doggish scent.

"Okay, let's let this brave little lady rest. We need to go run a couple tests."

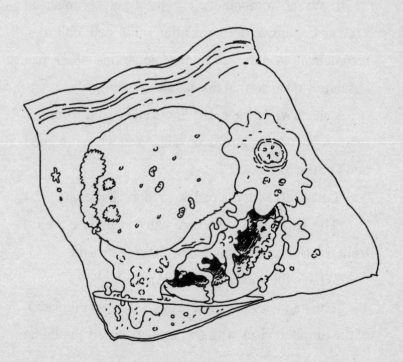

They left Madison alone and walked to a lab table equipped with a microscope, test tubes, and scales, all sparkling in the white fluorescent light. Dr. Scott snapped on a pair of latex gloves. She took the BurgerDog specimen and scraped off some samples into a petri dish. She then added a green liquid. She added some of Rice's ginkgo biloba and mixed it all together.

They listened intently as Dr. Scott explained her hypothesis.

It was all antibodies, T cells, base serums and vaccines, passive immunization and cell cultures, recombinant vectors and mutagenic strains—Zack had absolutely no idea what this lady was talking about.

A short while later, Dr. Scott looked up from her microscope. "All right," she said. "You want the good news or the bad news?"

"Let's start with the bad news, doc," Zack said.

"The bad news is that we can't formulate a cure from the BurgerDog specimen alone," she said.

"What's the good news?" Rice asked.

"The good news is that through the recombination of the mutated virus with the antiserum, we should be able to cultivate once the phytotoxins morph with the antibodies . . . and blah blah blah."

Zack's eyes glazed over as Dr. Scott's medical jargon turned into a series of droning blahs.

" . . . blah blah . . . but if one of us ingests the original virus, then we could potentially harvest the antigenic protein complex from the biogenetic mutation, which is blah blah blah, and could save us all."

"So . . . someone here has to actually eat that stuff?" Zoe asked, gleaning the gist.

"Precisely." The doctor jotted something down in a logbook.

Zack furrowed his brow in confusion. *That's the good news?*

"Well, I can't do it," Zoe asserted.

"Why not?" Zack said.

"Because I can't turn back into a zombie," she said. "Hah!"

"And I can't eat it," said Dr. Scott. "I'm the only one who knows how to concoct the antidote."

"Looks like it's just you and me." Rice clapped a hand on his buddy's shoulder.

There was a long silence before anyone spoke.

"There's only one way to settle this," Zack announced.

"Best of three?" Rice asked.

Zack nodded.

And so commenced the highest-stakes game of Rock-Paper-Scissors ever played. "One-two-three, shoot!" Both of them threw Rock. Followed by another Rock . . . and another.

"Stop doing Rock!" Zack shouted.

"You stop it!" Rice yelled back.

"One-two-three, shoot!"

Zack's Paper covered Rice's Rock.

"One-two-three, shoot!"

Rice's Rock smashed Zack's Scissors.

"One to one," Rice said.

There was a long hesitation, as the two friends stared at each other, flaring their nostrils.

"One-two-three, shoot!" They did the two Rocks thing, three more times.

"Shoot!"

Zack threw Rock for the fourth time, caught up in

the quadruple-reverse psychology. Rice held his hand flat over his buddy's fist—Paper. Rice dropped to his knees and threw up his arms as though he had just won a Grand Slam tennis tourney. "Eat that!"

"No." Dr. Scott handed the BurgerDog to Zack. "Eat this." The good doctor stood close at hand, ready to administer the last available dose of Madison's blood.

Zack's stomach dropped as he looked down at the diseased piece of disgusting fast food. The bun was soggy and growing mold, and a spiral clump of hair clung to the patty. The clumpy pistachio-green mayo relish smelled like rotten raw chicken.

"Doc, are you sure about this?" Zack asked skeptically.

"It's our only chance," she told him.

Zack looked at his sister helplessly. She shrugged. "He won fair and square, Zack."

Zack lifted the lethal sandwich slowly to his mouth and sunk his teeth into the burbling meat patty. He chewed as fast as possible, trying hard not to gag it

back up. Tears streamed down his face as he choked down the viral fast food.

He gulped a second time and then a third.

A massive head rush made him immediately nauseous.

Zack looked at the skin on the back of his hand. It grew rough and crinkly, aging eighty years in an eyeblink.

All of a sudden his vision became blurry, and he could barely see. He could hear the blood beating through his head. He started to hyperventilate. His lungs stopped pumping air. He couldn't breathe. There was a flash of red, and then everything went completely black as his eyeballs rolled back into their sockets.

Zack's final thought before he collapsed was, *I should have thrown Scissors.*

CHAPTER 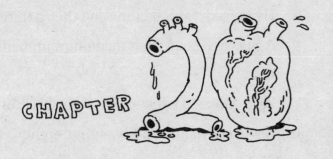 20

ack woke up sitting in a wheelchair. He was rolling fast down a long corridor. The White House was raging out of control, teeming with undead fiends. He blinked his eyes a few times to rule out the chance that he was dreaming.

"Code blue, code blue," a walkie-talkie crackled. "All White House personnel are instructed to evacuate immediately! The enemy has invaded. Repeat: The enemy has invaded!"

Zack felt a fat, swollen lump on his cheekbone, and the skin on his hand had a pale green tint. Crazed zombies staggered out of doorways, pouring around every corner.

Five yards directly in front of him, Ozzie hopped along on a pair of crutches, rocking a big cast on his right leg. Zack turned around in the rollicking seat. Rice was pushing the wheelchair through the gurgling zombie chaos.

"Yo, Zack . . . you're back!" Rice shouted happily.

"What's going on?" Zack asked, shouting over the noise.

"Watch out!" Rice swerved the wheelchair, dodging a flailing zombie construction worker in a yellow hard hat.

Ozzie whacked the zombie down with the rubber butt of his crutch. He spun, one-footed, and unleashed a staggering roundhouse kick with the cast on his leg, bashing another undead ghoul in the dome.

Zack looked to his right. Madison was drifting in and out of consciousness as Dr. Scott pushed her in a wheelchair. Zoe ran next to them carting the IV stand.

"Did it work?" Zack asked his buddy.

"Yeah, it worked." Rice chuckled.

Dr. Scott reached into the breast pocket of her lab coat and pulled out a test tube of red serum corked with a pink rubber plug.

Ozzie bashed through a couple more zombies as they reached the elevator, the only exit. Zack leaned over in his wheelchair and pushed the UP button three times, fast. They waited, huffing and puffing, for the elevator to arrive.

Bing! The doors opened, and they piled into the elevator car. Just then, Dr. Scott let out a terrifying screech. A zombie secretary had latched on to her back and was gnawing at her neck cords.

"Oww!" Dr. Scott spun around in a circle, trying to shuck the crazed mutant off her back.

The zombie flew off Dr. Scott's shoulder and smashed into the wall. The doctor jerked back, reeling in pain, which sent the vial of antidote springing out of her pocket.

"Nooooooo!" everyone shouted, eyes wide, mouths frozen in ovals of disbelief.

Time slowed as the precious serum floated up, hung for a moment, and then fell back down.

Rice dove in slow motion out of the elevator car, his hands outstretched as if he were a wide receiver diving for an overthrown football. The antidote dropped out of reach, just past his fingertips, and went crashing to the floor.

Zack grabbed his forehead involuntarily.

But the test tube didn't smash. It wasn't made of glass.

Rice wiped his brow and crawled on hands and knees toward the plastic serum vial, but not fast enough. A zombie foot kicked the antidote down the hall, sending it into the shuffling riff-raff.

Zack leaped out of the wheelchair and ran past Rice, jumping up to kick the zombie's noggin like a soccer

ball. The beast collapsed in a pile of slimy, decomposing mush.

Zack darted forward into the zigzagging zombie madness and snagged the vial as the zombie horde bulldozed up the hallway. He raced away from the undead swarm and pulled his buddy to his feet.

Zack and Rice sprinted back toward the elevator, which Ozzie held open with his crutch. Dr. Scott leaned down on one knee, clutching her collarbone. A deep red bloodstain was spreading over the shoulder of her white lab coat.

"Come on!" Zack slung her in the empty seat of the wheelchair and hit the CLOSE DOOR button. The zombies were only three feet away, jolting and sputtering flecks of infectious goop. A fat zombie man fell forward, stretching its arm out of its socket to reach them. Its liver-spotted wrist dropped into the gap between the closing doors.

The doors reopened.

Zack kicked the rotting zombie hand back into the hallway and hit the button once again. The ghoul rose to its feet slowly. Behind it, a sickening duo—two zombie women with tattoos and shredded black leather

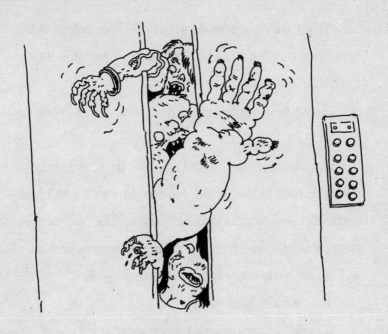

jackets—growled and lunged for the packed elevator. The biker chicks collided with the pot-bellied brute and tumbled in a gruesome heap of puckered flesh.

The doors finally closed, and the elevator rose.

Sitting in the wheelchair, Dr. Scott pressed the wet, bloody wound on her shoulder.

"Here." Zack handed her the vial. "Just take a tiny sip."

"Save the others first," she whispered sternly. The veins on her face bulged and pulsed. Her skin was pale and ashen. "It's up to you kids."

"What are we gonna do with her?" Rice asked as Dr. Scott's eyes rolled back in her head and her skin began to bubble with boils.

"Bring her," Zack said. "We'll save her as soon as we can."

The elevator doors opened, and they stepped out onto the roof of the White House. The sky was black and spangled with twinkling stars. The storm had cleared, but the zombies raged on, pouring out of a stairwell door on the other side of the roof.

"Now what?" asked Zoe.

"There!" Ozzie pointed to a chopper.

The helicopter that had brought Madison to the White House was halfway across the deck.

"Can you fly that thing, too?" Zack asked.

Ozzie furrowed his brow. "*Please. . . .*" He scoffed then smiled.

The zombies on the roof grabbed greedily at the air, making *nom-nom* noises, and Zack noticed General Munschauer and Agent Gustafson thrashing in the zombified bunch.

"Come on!" Rice shouted. "Quick!"

Rice and Zoe raced across the roof deck and loaded Madison, Twinkles, and the zombifying doctor into the executive helicopter, and climbed in after them. Ozzie hopped behind the navigation controls. Zack sat in the copilot seat.

Ozzie pressed a few buttons and hit a few switches. "Helicopters are a piece of cake," he said.

Cake? Zack thought about the pulsing BurgerDog sandwich, and for the first time all day, he wasn't the least bit hungry.

The propeller rotated slowly, and the rotors started to chop, churning the air into a wild wind that flattened the treetops.

The helicopter leaped off the rooftop in one smooth *whoosh* and they rose at an angled tilt over the rain-drenched streets of Washington, D.C. The zombie footsloggers raged furiously through the monuments, memorials, and museums below.

Zack pulled the vial of serum out of his pocket and stared at it. He turned around, looking in the back of the chopper. Madison rubbed noses with Twinkles. Zoe had tied up Dr. Scott and put a gas mask over her face. Rice looked excitedly at Zack.

"Dude." He smirked. "You were a freakin' zombie!"

"*Nom nom nom*," Zoe gurgled, making zombie noises. "*Braaaaains!*" She laughed.

"What can I say, Zo?" Zack shrugged. "I've always wanted to be just like you."

"Who doesn't?" The unzombified siblings smiled at each other.

And the chopper shot low through the East Coast night, chasing the westward sunset on its way back to Phoenix.

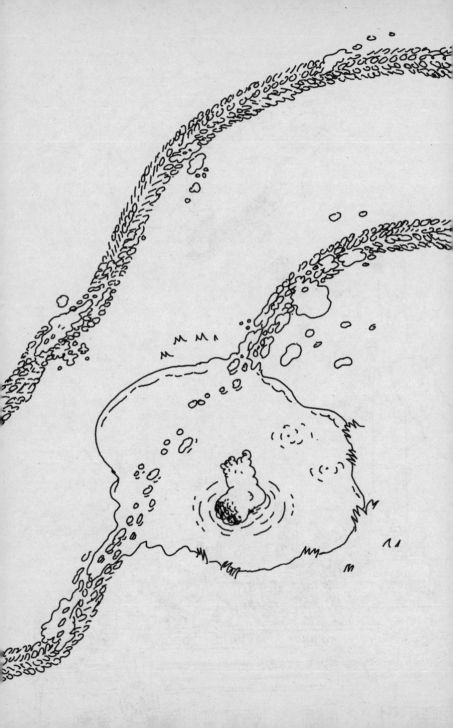

What brain-gobbling ghouls will
the Zombie Chasers battle next?

Turn the page for a sneak peek at
the next ZOMBIE CHASERS novel,

CHAPTER 1

The black Secret Service helicopter jetted under the clouds as a sea of the walking dead ravaged the landscape below.

Inside the chopper, Zack Clarke stared out the curved windshield, watching the full moon vanish from the sky then reappear like a magician's coin trick. It was late. Or was it early? Zack had been losing track of time since the zombie outbreak on Friday night. It was Sunday now, and he was exhausted, hopelessly praying for the moment when he would wake up from this zombie nightmare, back in his own room in Arizona. But that wasn't going to happen. That was one thing he knew for sure.

Zack was riding shotgun next to Ozzie in the cockpit of the helicopter they had commandeered back at the White House. His sister, Zoe; her BFF, Madison Miller; Zack's best buddy, Rice; and Doctor Scott, the ginkosedated zombie scientist, were all resting in the back of the chopper. Madison's puppy, Twinkles, snored contently in her lap.

"Where are we now?" Zoe asked, her voice a little weary.

Ozzie pointed to a red radar blip blinking over a neon green map of North America. "Near Memphis, Tennessee." An orange light ticked on the control board, and Ozzie's eyes flicked down to the fuel gauge. He shifted the levers and hit a few buttons. The chopper began to descend.

"Gotta gas up," Ozzie explained as they cruised just above the treetops.

Zack gazed out the cockpit window as they flew over a used car lot and some fast food joints, angling toward a glowing Shell gas station sign, which was missing its first letter.

Ozzie lowered the chopper to the rooftop over the fuel pumps, and they touched down.

"Why are we landing up here?" Zack asked.

"Better to stay above ground level," Ozzie said. "Come on, we gotta do this quick." Ozzie grabbed his crutches off the floor and then leaped from the cockpit with his one good leg.

Zack hopped onto the flat gravelly roof and stared out at the view. The night was pitch-black, but the darkness was alive with the moans and howls of the living dead.

Rice and Zoe jumped from the chopper, too, and threw the rope ladder off the side of the roof. Ozzie climbed down first. Zoe looked at Rice and gestured for him to go ahead.

3

"Ladies first," she said.

Rice made a face and climbed down after Ozzie.

Zack followed his sister, edging backward nervously until he found one of the rungs with his foot. *Here we go again* . . . , he thought, wobbling twenty feet in the air. Zack's feet hit the ground and he let out a grunt. He scanned the darkened perimeter. No zombies in sight, but the stink of death and decay filtered through his nostrils. He squinted into the blackness, and then the shadows came slowly into focus as the zombies tottered toward the dim neon glow of the gas station.

Rice put his hand on Zack's shoulder. "I see dead people," he whispered.

"Listen up," Ozzie barked. Then he slammed something into Zack's chest. "Buy us a little time with these flares while—" He cut himself off, pointing to a stack of red gas containers by the storefront sidewalk. "Zoe, gimme your mom's credit cards and bring those over here!"

"Excuse me, Mr. Bossypants." Zoe flung the handbag at him and darted toward the red gas jugs. All around them the zombies were closing in, their arms wide open, lips shriveled back, barking mucus and sputtering phlegm.

"Ready?" Rice held out his fist. Zack gave Rice a triple pound. They lit the flares and then took off in opposite directions.

Straight ahead, an elderly zombie gentleman lumbered toward Zack.

"Hey!" Zack called out to the slobbering old codger. The zombie sneered back at him, revealing its hideous decomposing chompers. A nasty boil exploded like a lava bubble. "This way, mister!" Zack waved the flare back and forth, jogging side to side, diverting the growing throng of zombies away from Ozzie and Zoe at the gas pumps.

"Ahhhhhh!" Rice shouted as he lost control of his zombie flock.

Zack whipped his head around. An undead biker in a black leather vest grabbed Rice's leg and yanked him onto the asphalt.

"Rice!" Zack shouted. But he could only watch as his best friend was swallowed up by the ravenous mob.

Zack felt sick to his stomach. He turned away, dizzy with grief.

But just then, out of the corner of his eye, he spotted his friend crawling on all fours out of the massive undead pile-on. With glasses askew, Rice scrabbled to his feet and lit another flare. He then struck a fencing stance and galloped in place like a medieval swordsman. "En garde!"

Zack had just breathed a sigh of relief when all of a sudden a terrified screech rang out from above. *Madison!* Twinkles was barking crazily overhead, and Zack could see the zombified doctor thrashing around inside the helicopter. He spun away from the zombie front line and raced for the rope ladder.

"Aahhhhhh!" Madison's voice shrieked in desperation. And without a second thought, Zack scrambled back up the ladder, hoping he wasn't too late.

Want to read the rest of

SLUDGMENT DAY ?

Find out more at
thezombiechasers.com

Thank you

ACKNOWLEDGMENTS

I would like to thank Sara Shandler, Josh Bank, Rachel Abrams, Elise Howard, and Lucy Keating for all of their hard work and indispensable zombie wisdom; Steve Wolfhard for his wonderfully gory illustrations; and Kristin Marang and Liz Dresner for putting together a fantastic website.

I would also like to thank my friends and family for their support, and for not turning into zombies during the writing of this book.

—J. K.